GEM HUNTER

A NOVELLA

JANICE BOEKHOFF

GEM HUNTER

JANICE BOEKHOFF

Published by:

Lost Canyon Press

P.O. Box 283

Prairieville, LA 70769

978-1-948003-01-8 Trade Paperback ISBN

978-1-948003-00-1 eBook ISBN

Book Cover Design by Kim Mesman (kmgrapics1.carbonmade.com)

ONE

At the sharp yank on the back of his prison jumpsuit, Ruger Westmoreland whipped around, arms curled, fists clenched, ready to fight.

"Afraid you won't make it out of here alive?" Jared chuckled.

Ruger scowled at his brother's accurate guess. Even though Ruger was scheduled for release in two days, part of him believed this place would reach out with slithering chains and drag him back into the depths of depravity. His time at Central Colorado State Prison couldn't end soon enough.

A muscular inmate with an intricate tattoo on his bicep passed within ten yards of them. Jared gave the man a warning glare. The man winked and sauntered to the other side of the prison yard. The rest of the men in the yard ignored them. Somehow, Jared garnered respect even in this crowd. Ruger had only survived in here because of him. Even so, Ruger's gratitude was constantly diluted by the injustice of being here. The least Jared could do was protect him.

"Hey, bro, I need to talk to you." Jared moved to put his back against the interior prison wall, his eyes tracking the movements of the general population.

Ruger moved to the spot next to Jared and he, too, stared out at the inmates. Some huddled in small groups, others loudly recounted the glory of their days on the outside, and others simply walked on the green grass, paying no notice to the barbed-wire-topped concrete wall that separated them from the real world.

"I need you to do something for me."

"The last time you said that, I ended up here." The familiar pulse of anger shot through him, but he pushed it down with practiced ease and kept his voice neutral. For the next two days, Jared was still his lifeline. "What is this about?"

An uncomfortable shifting on the wall. If Jared was nervous, this was bad. "Before I came to prison, I did something horrible."

Ruger let his shoulders slump forward. "Duh."

Jared shook his head. "Not that. Something worse."

Something worse than embezzlement? Silence fell over them as Ruger tried to guess what Jared meant. *Maybe he's just messing with me.*

As the prisoners in the yard grew louder, the silence between them dragged on. An old fear rose up, forming a hard knot in Ruger's throat. He might know exactly what his brother had done, but he couldn't ask. Not in this place. Not when he lived or died based on Jared's protection.

Jared pushed off the wall and turned to face Ruger, allowing Ruger to watch his back, a message of trust. "I know I have no right to ask this..." The muscle under Jared's left eye twitched. To cause such stress in Ruger's normally rock-steady brother, whatever this was had to be illegal. "I need you to get rid of something for me."

Ruger folded his arms over his chest. "What?"

"Evidence."

Tampering with evidence would land Ruger back in prison. How could Jared ask that? He knew what it felt like to fear the next hour, the next moment. To go to bed terrified each night and wake up to a nightmare every day. And yet, somehow the fear didn't tie Jared up in knots like it did Ruger.

Jared lowered his eyes briefly, then raised them, his brows arched, his mouth parted in a pleading expression. "The less you know, the better. For your own protection. I just need you to pick up a box and dump it in a lake or drop it down a mine shaft. Put it somewhere deep."

For your own protection. Like the day Jared had kept Ruger in the dark and gotten him arrested. Ignorance hadn't helped him then. "Tell me what's in it."

"Believe me, you don't want to know. I'm just afraid someone will find it."

"I'm not going after it if I don't know what's in it."

Jared nodded quickly as though Ruger's refusal was inconsequential. "It's buried in the old cave we used to play in. Do you remember?"

"Yeah." Ruger unfolded his arms and wiped his hands on his pants. "But I don't think I can find it."

A forced chuckle escaped Jared's lips. "You were always better with directions than me. You'll find it."

Irritation simmered in Ruger's chest. Jared assumed he'd go, assumed everyone would do his bidding. Worst part was, they usually did.

"Come on, bro." Jared swept an arm toward the prison yard. "You know I've taken care of you."

Ruger shifted his gaze to a scuffle between two meaty inmates in the far corner. The other inmates cast interested glances at the pair, waiting to see if it would develop into a real brawl. Just like his first time in the yard when a hulking bald inmate had shoved him to the ground. Everyone else stood around watching, expecting a battle, albeit a minor one since Ruger was no match for the guy. Until Jared came to stand behind him. Not wanting to fight the two of them, the man left after a swift kick to Ruger's stomach. The next day, Ruger heard rumors of the bald man being taken to the infirmary. Somehow, he'd broken that same leg after a fall in the hallway. Probably a coincidence, but since then, no one had dared to pick a fight with the Westmoreland brothers.

Jared prodded Ruger with an elbow. "So you'll take care of this for me."

That was Jared. The older brother by five years, but always asking Ruger to take care of things. At least in prison Jared had returned the favor.

After another nudge from Jared's elbow, Ruger nodded, silently asking God to forgive the lie. He had no intention of following his brother's commands. Jared wasn't due to get out for several more years, so he wouldn't know what Ruger did or didn't do. And if he did go after the box, it wouldn't be to destroy evidence. It would be to keep Jared right where he was.

TWO

Alyna Elkins stumbled, catching herself just before she plummeted off the sharp cliff. After regaining her footing, she pushed her way up the steep rocky slope, savoring the crunch of rock under her boots. This wasn't the easiest way to get to her claim, but she couldn't afford to leave a well-worn path for others to follow. She hitched her backpack up and kept climbing, leaving small rocks to tumble downslope with every step.

About halfway up, she stopped and scanned the slope below. A tingle skipped down her spine. Unaccustomed to the feeling of being watched out here, she searched the sea of trees. She and her partner, Quin Lynch, had gotten through almost the entire prospecting season with no problems. Surely her imagination had jumped into overdrive. She shifted her gaze above the tree line to the rugged peak of Mt. Antero, the mountain nearest to her Mt. Pasaqua claim. Nobody, and yet the feeling of being watched persisted.

She flipped her backpack off and unhooked her rifle from the bungee cord straps. She held it up and chambered a round. The clicking sound echoed off the surrounding rocks. That should be enough to let anyone who might be out there know she wasn't easy prey. Maybe she should have brought Quin with her for the morning, but he needed to pack for his trip. He'd already given most of his summer break from teaching helping her dig up only a few gemstones. She couldn't ask any more of him.

She pointed the rifle toward the ground, hefted her pack, and continued the climb. If her instincts were right, fighting off a claim jumper would be a rough ending to the year, but she had to finish strong. Their total take of aquamarine gemstones from the summer wasn't even close to enough to fund her winter plans.

At the top of the slope, the ground leveled off into a plateau. Behind the flat rocks, a spire stretched out to touch the sky. Under the spire, or more like inside it, lay a thin vein of aquamarine—their claim. The long orange spike marking it as theirs hadn't moved.

She shrugged off her pack again, dropping it on the ground. Something wasn't right. Scuff marks and shoe prints marred the area. More of them than she would expect. She moved slowly forward until she found a distinct set of footprints, then held her foot next to them. They were huge. A size or two bigger than both hers or Quin's.

A claim jumper. *Ugh. It stinks to be right.*

Tightening her grip on the rifle, she surveyed the area. The prints looked random enough. Maybe the claim jumper didn't know what to look for. Lots of amateurs came up here expecting to find gems lying on the surface, then left quickly when they discovered prospecting for gems—the backbreaking work of digging them out of the rock—wasn't easy or a get-rich-quick endeavor.

After another visual search of the area, Alyna grabbed a water bottle and a small rock pick, then circled around to the far side of the spire. The vein was hidden inside a split seam of rock that formed a cave barely big enough to fit a person. For the last week, Alyna had squeezed in to chip away at the matrix. She'd pulled out several five-carat aquamarines and a dozen smaller ones. Another few months with discoveries like this and her archeological research would be completely funded, except the prospecting season was almost over. Soon, the fall storms would drive her from the mountain. The last thing she needed at this point was a jumper stealing all her profits.

She'd have to take care of this guy the old-fashioned way, which meant she needed supplies from camp. She snagged her pack and headed down the mountain in a different direction. Let whoever might be watching think that nothing was up here. At least, until she got back.

The mile-long hike back to camp dragged on. She'd much rather be searching for aqua on her claim than dealing with theft. But thieves came with the isolated nature of the Rocky Mountains. Thankfully, not many of them knew that Mt. Pasaqua had any aqua claims on it. Mt. Antero was more popular due to its easily accessible roads.

As she pushed through the last group of trees, she found Quin zipping his tent shut.

His shaggy dark hair flipped about as he stood. "Hey, Al, what are you doing back so soon?"

"I saw strange tracks at the site. Looks like we've got a claim jumper."

He shook his head. "We almost made it through the season."

"At least they left our claim marker alone."

Quin grabbed the loop on his backpack, letting it dangle over the ground in one hand. "Do you want me to stay and help you deal with it? It is my claim, after all."

She smiled and shook her head at his teasing tone. The land where the claim sat belonged to the father of someone Quin knew in high school. He might have arranged the deal for the mining rights, but she worked the land more faithfully than he did. In the end, they would split the profits equally. "No, I just need to set out a nasty welcome mat. The stuff is in my car."

"Okay. I'll walk with you. Your mom is picking me up along the road."

"Oh yeah." She'd forgotten that her mom had offered to drive Quin back to town. Usually Quin had his own car, but his mom's car had died, so he'd left it with her until she could get hers fixed. Alyna hesitated before following him into the woods. Depending on her mood, Mom could either be as docile as a sleeping rabbit or as hyped up as a squirrel. Even so, Alyna needed the stuff from her car. "Are you excited to see your mom for the weekend?"

Quin shot her a look. She laughed as she led the way through the woods. "Your sister won't even be there."

"No, but that means I have to listen to my mom complain about Bridezilla, and that's almost worse."

"Hey, cut your baby sister a little slack. A wedding is a big deal."

He snorted. "Baby is right, but you know it's not just the wedding. She's always like this. Now she has an excuse to get really awful."

"It's so hard to deal with younger siblings." The sarcasm dripped from her words. She would love to have that problem. It had only ever been her and her parents. Then, as of four years ago, just her and Mom.

Quin caught up to walk beside her, holding branches back for her. "Debbie isn't so young. Same age as you, and you don't act like an emotional bag of neediness."

Putting a hand over her heart, she said, "I'll take that as a compliment." Except it probably wasn't true. Her own mess drove her on the inside. She just didn't share it with anyone. Not even Quin.

They arrived at the road to find her mother already waiting.

Mom's slender fingers tapped on the steering wheel impatiently. The gesture didn't bode well for her mood.

Alyna gave Mom a friendly smile before opening the trunk of her own car. She rummaged through the random contents until she found half of a spool of wire and a canister of black powder. When she turned around, Mom was waving her over. She approached the car warily.

Mom put on her sunny church smile. Maybe Alyna had misjudged her mood. "Dear, why don't you come home for the weekend too? No need to stay out here by yourself."

Alyna fought to hold back an eye roll. Her mom *never* wanted her to be out here. Plus, they'd had this discussion last week when she came into town for supplies. "We've only got a few days left in the season. If it's nice out, I need to be working."

"But you don't have to do this. You've always loved kids. Principal Hedlund just told me they're looking for a history teacher and a math teacher. You're great at both of those."

She glanced over at Quin, who gave her a subtle shrug. He taught history at the high school and hadn't mentioned the job openings. She gave him a sweet smile for knowing she didn't want to teach and respecting that.

Turning back to Mom, she chewed on the inside of her cheek. At least this time Mom had brought a better job possibility than the usual position at the hardware store. "I can't do any archeology during the winter if I'm a teacher."

"My point exactly. Then you wouldn't leave for five months to Italy, and you wouldn't need to be out here next summer."

"I would still come out here every summer, even if I didn't need to."

Mom shook her head. "A girl should have some stability. Not this crazy life. You're out here wandering around, and you don't even know what you're looking for."

Right this minute, she was looking to get rid of her mother, but she wouldn't say so. Respect for her elders and such. She clamped her mouth shut, waiting for her mother to finish. Hopefully soon.

"It's just reckless for you to be out here alone."

Alyna hefted up the rifle as a show of her ability to protect herself.

"You know it's not just me who thinks your gem hunting is a bad idea. I had a long talk with Pastor Walker the other day. As Christians, we're supposed to use our time to help others to know Jesus. All you're doing is hiding away on a mountain."

Great. Now Mom had spiritual objections to gem hunting. More fuel for the fire.

"If you keep following this crazy life..." Mom pressed her hands together and bit her lip, as though she was afraid of what she was about to say. "I'm afraid you'll end up like your father."

How dare she bring Dad into this. "I'm done talking." Alyna walked away, heading back down the hill. Behind her, a car door opened, then slammed shut. Footsteps sounded and a hand grabbed her arm, twisting her around. But it wasn't her mother. Quin squinted at her, pity etching lines in his face.

"You okay?"

"Yeah. I've...uh." The claim jumper flashed through her mind. "I've got to get back to set things up."

"You're sure you don't want me to stay?" Quin ran his hand down her arm.

The gesture should have comforted her, but her nerves were frayed. She took a step back. "No. I'll be fine." And she would be, after a few rants that only the grizzly bears could hear.

Quin twisted his lips like he wanted to say something, but then he nodded and walked back to the car. She caught a glimpse of her mother, head resting on the steering wheel. A guilty posture? More likely one of frustration.

Alyna turned away and trudged down the hill toward the

claim site. An hour later, she'd finished her aimless ranting and arrived at the claim with her emotions mostly under control. She was ready to work.

The neon orange claim-marker spike still stood at the edge of the slope. A quick peek inside the cave showed nothing amiss. Turning sideways, she scooted through the opening and delved to the far end of the crack about five feet inside. This was the only time in her life when being china-doll sized worked in her favor.

She pulled from her backpack a length of wire and eye hooks. She bent down to hammer in the eye hooks, then looped the nearly invisible wire across the cavern entrance at ankle height. The claim jumper would trip and fall, giving her time to get her gun.

With her warning system in place, she spent several hours tapping her rock pick against the granite, extracting light blue, clear crystals of aquamarine. Most of them in this area were small, but numerous. Even so, she'd love to find a museum-quality piece.

Every time she came out to stretch, she carried the rifle with her and scanned the area, looking for any sign of people. The feeling of being watched had subsided and all seemed quiet. At about three o'clock, the sunlight started to fade. The days were getting shorter, and the mountains blocked the sun well before it set at night. Time to quit for the day and leave a surprise for the claim jumper.

On one end, just to the side of the entrance, she attached the wire to a small canister of black powder. Anyone who disturbed her claim tonight would regret it. The blast wouldn't be fatal, but the thief would likely run off with some burns.

As she surveyed her work, meant to harm an unknown enemy, her mom's words came back, floating through her head. *You'll end up like your father.* Her mom meant it as a warning.

Maybe Alyna had gone a little off the deep end by planning to go to Italy, but she refused to leave her father's life unfinished.

Alyna startled awake, instinctively reaching for the rifle next to her sleeping bag. Enough moonlight filtered through the canvas walls to reassure her no one was in the tent. Everything was exactly as she'd left it. The rifle had been by her side. Her laptop rested on the other side of her with the black jump drive sticking out of the side. She'd forgotten to put the drive away after saving a backup of her spreadsheet detailing the gemstones she'd found along with their location and possible value. Her rock pick still sat above her head, an extra weapon just in case. It was all good.

So what had woken her? A faint echo reverberated against the rocky cliffs. She mentally replayed the first few seconds before she'd come to complete consciousness. A muffled boom, probably from the east.

Realization crept into her cloudy mind. Someone had tripped her booby trap.

Still clutching the rifle, Alyna threw a coat over her pajamas, her boots on her feet, and dashed out into the dark. When she reached the slope leading to the claim, all was quiet. She switched off her flashlight, letting her eyes adjust. No movement came from above.

She flipped the flashlight back on and quickly climbed the slope, switching it off again at the top. Tiny tendrils of smoke, bright white in the darkness, drifted from behind the spire, disappearing in the light breeze. With cautious steps, she circled around to the cave entrance. Even in the dark the edges of the cave stood out as blackened against the light-colored granite.

No sound. Nothing to indicate anyone was still around. Satisfied it was safe, she flipped the flashlight back on and scanned the small cave. The canister of black powder lay a foot in front of the entrance. The blast had projected out, just as she'd planned, saving her work area. But had a person or animal tripped it?

She shined the light down at her feet. A few unknown footprints were pressed into the gravel, large ones with the same tread as what she'd seen yesterday. No animal tracks anywhere.

Bending down, she directed the light at the wire still stretched across the entrance. A thin sheen of red coated one side. Blood.

Surely the person had worn long pants. The evening temperatures this late in the summer were around 40 degrees Fahrenheit.

Her eyes locked on to another spot of red near the right side of the entrance. Small drops of blood tinged the end of a sharp piece of granite. When the intruder tripped the trap, the explosion must have hurled the small chunk of granite into one of the person's legs. That would hurt for a while.

She smiled. The claim jumper had gotten more than he'd bargained for. At least he wouldn't likely come back tonight. She'd reset the trap tomorrow. As she made her way back down the slope, she kept her flashlight moving in wide circles all throughout the trees. If this person was anywhere around, she wanted to know.

THREE

The sun woke Alyna with its insistent brightness after she'd slept a few more hours. She'd never had much luck sleeping during the day. Fighting off the grogginess, she dressed and walked back to her car for another canister of black powder. She'd have to make this next trap more challenging, in case the claim jumper was the persistent type, otherwise he would know now to unhook the wire. Most people would give up after the first explosion, but she couldn't count on that.

Two hours later, she slid into the cave sideways to survey the damage. Blackened walls toward the entrance, but the aquamarine vein was intact. *Thank you, God, for protecting my investment.* She and Quin had each paid a thousand dollars up front to mine this area for the season. So far, they had barely made a profit. She couldn't afford to take even one day off if she wanted to continue Dad's research this winter.

She knelt and whacked the bottom portion of the vein with her rock pick. A few ordinary chunks of granite broke off. She raised the pick for another strike, then stopped.

Something on the side wall caught her eye. A dark brown

circular area in the midst of the blackened rock. She'd missed it because the colors blended in the shadows of the cave. A layer of dust coated the floor on that side. The explosion must have uncovered it last night. She grabbed her flashlight to get a better look.

What would cause such discoloration? Her training was in archeology, not specifically geology, so the nuances of rock composition sometimes eluded her, but this didn't appear natural. She shuffled over a few paces and scratched at the brown layer with the wider end of her pick. Several pieces flaked off and fell to the ground. They were laminar and crumbly, not like rock at all.

She picked a piece up and rubbed her fingers across it. It broke up into long tubular splinters. She lifted a larger piece, peering close in the dim light. Decomposing wood. *How in the world did it get here?*

She continued scraping. The decomposing fibers fell off to reveal harder wood. A box maybe? As her pick fought to free the object from the granite, she noticed the area a few inches around it gave way easier. Either someone had carved out the granite to fit the object in or they had placed it in a natural cavity.

With the sharp end of her pick, she followed the line of the object about ten inches along the bottom. Then it made a right-angle turn up the side. Straight sides with right angles between. She couldn't see how deep it went into the rock, but now she was sure it was a box.

After she had loosened the material around it, she grabbed a crevice tool and began to pry it out. She worked the tool up and down on the top and bottom until the box slid from its rocky tomb.

The first layer of wood on the side that had been facing her crumbled a little more, but the integrity of the box remained. The other three sides weren't decomposed at all. She stared in surprise as the front of the box came out of the cavity. Not only had someone buried it in the middle of nowhere, but they had secured it with a padlock. Why?

She tugged on the lock. It didn't budge. She peered at the metal plates through which the lock attached to the box. They were screwed into the wood. She could take the whole lock off with a screwdriver back at camp. But she would wait. As curious as she was about the contents, she needed to get in a full day of digging.

The hours stretched out. Every hour seemed like three while she kept glancing at the box in the corner. After a late lunch, she forced herself to work two more hours. By three o'clock, she could stand the suspense no longer.

She scooted out of the cave, pushing the box and her small collection of aqua crystals ahead of her. She almost raced down to camp without setting up another welcome surprise for the thief. But she couldn't leave her site unprotected. And the little opening left by the box was the perfect place to put the canister this time.

She grabbed several tree branches she'd cut earlier that day and placed them longways in front of the opening as a curtain. Selecting the third one in from the right, she attached the wire along the whole of the branch. Whoever came upon the site would sweep the branches away in one motion and trigger the explosion.

She checked that her rifle was attached to her pack, packed her loot inside, then picked up the box and headed down the mountain. The day was coming to a close, but she could still see the delicate flowers of hot pink fireweed dotting the valley and surrounding mountains. She drank in the tranquil sunset, letting her eyes roam at will, then her gaze froze to a single spot.

Movement on a ridge across the valley.

Willing her heartbeat to stay under control, she dropped the box on the ground and dug her binoculars out of her backpack. *It could be an animal.* She focused the lenses on the ridge. Tiny hairs jumped to attention on the back of her neck. She could barely make out the outline of a man standing amid the trees, wearing jeans and a dusty green flannel shirt. He looked in her direction before he disappeared into the foliage.

After scanning the trees for several more minutes, she gave up hoping for another look. She stuffed her binoculars back in her pack and headed downslope again.

At her campsite, she located a screwdriver. The screws holding in the locking plates proved especially tight, but she finally dislodged them enough to pull the lock off the box. Slowly, she lifted the lid, a sense of anticipation swelling in her chest. Other than stray beer bottles, she'd never found anything man-made at a claim site.

Inside, resting on a cream-colored cloth were numerous bright sparkling gemstones. The box was full of them. At least a dozen gem-grade stones had been polished on one side, left rough on the other. Beautiful chunks of beryl, tourmaline, topaz, and more. Oddly enough, none of them were aquamarine. In her astonishment, she tipped the box a little. The stones rolled around, bumping into each other with the sound of smacking pool balls.

She straightened the box, then laid it on her lap. The tourmaline caught her eye first. She rolled it in her hand to examine it. Amazing coloring for a watermelon tourmaline, the shades varied from green, to pink, to red in perfectly even bars. A flawless specimen, and yet the roughness of the rest of the stone spoke to its authenticity as a natural gemstone. She picked up the aquamarine and came up with the same conclusion. These weren't lab created. In her hands, she held an entire box of perfect gemstones. It would be worth tens of thousands of dollars to collectors. She let out a high-pitched whistle. These specimens could fund her entire year of research.

As she held the aquamarine in one hand, she glanced down at the box. The corner of the cloth had lifted and there was something underneath. Gently, she placed each stone on top of her sleeping bag, then turned back to the box to pull out the cloth. A piece of brown cardboard had been cut to fit the bottom. She snagged one end with her fingernail and yanked it out. Below it were two objects wrapped in cloth bags, a small one sitting on top of a larger one.

She grabbed the smaller one and carefully slid open the drawstring at the top, then tipped it into her palm. A flash drive fell out. Sleek and black, it looked just like the one she used in her laptop to back up her files. Why would somebody want to bury this? Maybe it had information on where the stones came from. She put it aside for later.

Next, she pulled out the larger sack. Whatever was inside felt slippery in her hand. After opening the drawstring, she peered inside. It was a smooth stone handle, but she couldn't see what the handle was for. She circled her fingers around it and tugged. The object came out easy for a few inches, then the rest of it got stuck. She pulled harder. The thin cloth fabric ripped as the rest broke free, torn by the blade of a six-inch knife.

A shudder went through her. She used knives at camp, but nothing like this. Had it been included in here because of the decorative stone handle?

She lay the knife on the bag in the bottom of the box and turned to stare at the rest of the contents on her sleeping bag. *How weird.* Who would want to bury such amazing stones? They should be on display in a museum or at least appreciated in a serious collector's home.

And what was with the flash drive? She picked it up, then dug her laptop out of her backpack. Resting the computer on her lap, she plugged in the drive just as a loud ringing filled the tent. The satellite phone. She stretched out her leg to drag the phone closer. When it came within arm's reach, she bent over and grabbed it.

"Hello."

"Hey, Al. I wasn't sure if you'd be in the tent this early, but I thought I'd try because I can't talk later."

She smiled at Quin's voice. "I was up at the claim, but came back early because I found something."

"Must have been a good specimen for you to want to clean it up and stash it in the safe right away."

More like good *specimens*, only she didn't collect them. "I haven't gotten them to the safe in the car yet, and they don't need to be cleaned up."

"They?"

"I found something buried in the rock. A wooden box with all kinds of amazing specimens inside."

"Wait. You're telling me I leave for one day, and you stumble on a buried treasure? No fair." His tone was teasing, as if he didn't believe her.

"I swear. It also had a flash drive and a knife."

"Seriously? Did you log it on your specimen spreadsheet?"

She rolled her eyes. He was still teasing. "Hey, I'm being serious. You're the one who's not listening."

Silence on the other end. When Quin finally spoke, he sounded more serious. "Well, the knife is creepy, but what's on the jump drive?"

"I don't know. I was just going to look. Hang on."

She woke her computer and clicked on the icon for the flash drive. A screen popped up.

Enter password.

"It's password-protected."

"Bummer. Now I'm really curious."

"Me too. Who do you think would have left it there?"

Quin made a soft tsking sound as he thought. "Maybe the owners leased the claim to someone else before us. Remember how rough the gem pocket looked when we started? Someone could have worked on it a little."

"I suppose."

"Well, no matter how it got there, it's ours now. Finders keepers. Take that, claim jumpers."

She stayed quiet as she thought of the man she'd spotted, the one who had probably set off the trap. But if she told Quin about him, Quin would insist on coming back. She didn't want to keep him from seeing his mom for the last week he had before school started.

"You haven't seen anyone yet, have you?"

He'd interpreted her silence too well. "Just from a distance." It was better not to tell him about the busted trap.

"Do you want me to come back?"

"No, I can handle myself."

He blew out a breath. "Keep your gun on you."

"No worries. I'll be fine."

"Okay, then." A voice yelled in the background. Quin's mom telling him that his popcorn was ready. They must have been ready to sit down to a movie. "I'll be right there," he called.

"Go enjoy your movie."

"Okay." A long pause before Quin's teasing voice came back over the line. "And you feel free to keep finding more of that buried treasure while I'm gone."

She gave a half-hearted laugh, then said goodbye. Finding the box shouldn't be such a big deal, but it meant everything to her. The chance to restore her father's reputation, to prove he wasn't crazy. The chance to change her mother's mind. The chance to use her archeology degree.

Alyna placed everything back inside, closed the lid, and

gripped the box with trembling fingers. As much as it meant to her, she couldn't shake the feeling that it had to be important to someone else also. For the first time, she wondered if the claim jumper was after the aquamarine at her claim site after all.

During the night, the dark woods seemed to have its own pulse, its own rhythm. Bats screeched overhead, leaves rustled, and bushes swayed with the stealthy movements of unknown creatures stalking their prey, or maybe it was the prey trying to escape. The area was just as Ruger remembered from the nights he and his brother had crept out of the house to go exploring. They would walk deep into the woods near their home several miles from here. Not the same location, but not so different from this place. If only Ruger were out for an easy evening of exploring tonight.

He bent at the waist and pushed a tree branch out of the way. Two tents sat in a small clearing. As far as he could tell, the one on the left was empty. The right one was hers.

A few hours ago, he'd seen a light glowing inside. Now it was as dark as a black hole. This could be his chance.

After disabling the second trap and searching everywhere in the high cave, he'd found nothing. Jared had said the box was in there, so whoever this woman was, she must have it with her.

He stepping into the clearing and waited a few heartbeats. No sound, no movement from within.

Moonlight filtered through the trees, sending long spirals of light shining down from above. He almost expected to see an alien mothership appear overhead, ready to beam him up. Man, this covert stuff was really taking a toll. On a different night, the gentle breeze and whisper of the trees would stir his soul. But look what Jared had turned him into—a stalker.

He approached the tent with silent steps, bent over, and gripped the zipper in two fingers. Slowly, he eased it back. It didn't make much noise as the canvas flap slid open. Placing the flap quietly on the ground, he peered inside.

The woman lay tucked in a sleeping bag, one arm out with her hand under her cheek. The moonlight gave her a pale glow. From a distance, he'd thought she'd be pretty, but up close, she was beautiful. Dark silky hair splayed across the tiny pillow. Even darker lashes rested on her cheeks. Her parted lips allowed the soft sound of her breathing to fill the tent. *Good.* Maybe she'd sleep through this entire violation of her space.

Tearing his eyes away from her, he scanned the inside of the tent. Nothing that resembled a box.

What if she'd hidden it somewhere else? Or reburied it? He might never find out why Jared wanted to destroy it. He sucked in a deep breath to calm his nerves.

Another scan of the tent gave him a glimpse of a sharp corner sticking out from under the sleeping bag. She'd gone to bed with it tucked beside her. His heart rate took off in a sprint. So much for not waking her.

He lifted his foot to enter, peering in to make sure nothing was below his feet. The only thing on the floor of the tent were some metal tools off to the side and a rifle near her head. He'd have to make sure she didn't wake and pick that up.

He stepped in.

A loud clanging sounded as the same tools crashed together. Another trip wire. Of course she'd have a trap on her tent. He should have checked more thoroughly.

As he tried to pull his foot out, it caught in the wire. Off-balance, he fell into the tent, twisting his body at the last second to keep from landing right on top of her.

The woman sat up and swung around, the rifle in her hand. Within one second, she had chambered a round. "Who are you?"

He froze, indecision warring within him. He probably shouldn't tell her the whole truth. *Yes, ma'am, don't mind me. I'm just a convicted felon who's been stalking you to steal what you just found in the cave.* That answer would get him shot. "Hi, my name is Ruger."

She raised her eyebrows and lifted one shoulder. "'Hi?' You broke into my tent in the middle of the night to say hi?"

"Sorry. It was the first thing that came to mind."

"What do you want?"

His newfound faith meant he should be honest. Besides, he couldn't seem to come up with another reason he'd be here. He'd just have to be gentle with his explanation. She brought the gun a few inches closer to his face. He raised his hands in the air. "Okay. I came for the box."

"Why?"

"It's my property."

Her glare told him she, rightfully so, didn't believe him. "And you couldn't just ask for it back?"

He'd thought of that and quickly dismissed the idea because he didn't want anyone to know he was out here, especially his dad. The guilty look on his face must have said it all, because she continued in a stern voice.

"So your last name is Benson?"

"What? No."

"Kyle Benson owns this land and I have mining rights to it. This box was found on my claim site, which makes it my property. If you had a legitimate claim to it, you should have come to me. As it is, I'm keeping the gems and taking the rest to the sheriff in the morning. If you have a claim to the gems, you can take up your case with him."

No. Not the sheriff. "Look, miss...I don't even know your name."

"Alyna," she grumbled.

"Alyna, I understand the situation, but I have to take the box now." He leaned behind her to grab it. This woman wouldn't really shoot him. He'd looked into the eyes of killers in prison, and she wasn't one.

She leaned back, blocking his reach. He moved forward, trying to get around her, but she held the rifle out sideways to make herself wider.

Stretching out, he almost grabbed the corner of the box once, but she smacked his arm with the butt of the gun. He grabbed the gun and wrenched it out of her hands. Her eyes widened with fear. He expected her to shrink away, but she lunged into the corner of the tent and came out with a wicked-looking hammer, some sort of rock pick.

She swung it full-force at his head.

He ducked, the sharp point narrowly missing his eye. Using the rifle as a shield against several more blows, he scooted toward the tent opening. Alyna lunged at him again, this time connecting with his thigh. He grunted in pain as he leapt through the flap, the gun still in his hands. That woman was crazy. He'd have to find another way to get the box. But one thing he knew for sure, he couldn't let her take it to the sheriff.

FOUR

The aching in her fingers woke Alyna. Her hand was latched on to the handle of her rock pick. She gently relaxed her fingers one by one. Hard to believe she'd actually fallen back asleep. After the incident during the night, she'd stayed awake as long as she could, staring at the tent entrance, the rock pick in her hand, determined not to be ambushed again.

The box! She stuck a hand under the pillow and felt the rough wood surface.

Pulling it into the light, she let out a sigh of relief. What was it about this box that made Ruger want it so badly?

She opened the lid and ran her fingertips over the beautiful gems. Did he plan to sell them? Better question: how had he even known they were there? Maybe they actually belonged to him. But thanks to her claim, she had rights to all minerals of value on this property. Would that include the ones in the box?

She'd take them to the sheriff today so he could figure out this mess, and then Ruger would leave her alone. And hopefully, the sheriff would also keep this quiet. If the incident last night got back to her mother, Alyna would never hear the end of how dangerous it was out here. Never mind that her mom may have a point. Alyna loved the deep woods, and when she'd needed to, she'd fought Ruger off. This was her claim site. No one would scare her away.

She placed the box on the floor of the tent and quickly changed out of her sweats and into jeans and a Colorado Rockies sweatshirt, before picking it back up. She rested the box on her lap and tugged out the thumb drive, leaving the knife where it lay on the bottom. What if this drive contained the locations where these gems were found? It would be a treasure trove, literally. If only she was better with computers, she'd try to crack the password herself.

Quin knew more about computers than she did. Maybe she'd save this one thing for him to take a look at. She'd found it on their claim site, after all, and if it pointed to more gems on the site, then she had a right to know. She could always take it to the sheriff later. Of course, she'd have a hard time arguing that a flash drive fell under the category of the mineral rights they'd purchased, but still she'd found it.

She slipped the flash drive into the front pocket of her jeans and closed the box. Keeping her rock pick in front of her, she cautiously opened the zippered entrance to the tent. All was quiet outside. She thanked God that Ruger hadn't come back. Circling around the tent, she went to the back of the clearing and brushed leaves off a two-foot-square area, revealing the buried safe she and Quin used to secure their most valuable finds. She spun the combination dial to open it, then pulled out her car keys and wallet.

She clutched the box to her chest as she trekked to her car. The mile hike took longer than normal because she stopped every few minutes to listen for sounds of anyone else in the woods.

The sight of her car brought a wave of relief. She climbed in, placed the box on the passenger's seat, and pushed the Start button.

Nothing happened.

She tried again, making sure her foot was on the brake pedal.

Still, nothing. Not even a flicker of life.

She popped the hood and climbed out to take a look. The battery was unhooked. She didn't know much about cars, but she knew enough to hook up the battery.

After adjusting the wires, she climbed back in and tried again.

The car whirred, but the engine didn't turn over.

She returned to the front and leaned under the hood. The jumble of parts and wires made no sense to her untrained eye. She had no idea what else might be wrong, but clearly someone didn't want her to leave.

A sour ball of dread swelled in her stomach. Only one person could have done this—Ruger.

Another frightening realization dawned. He'd known where her car was parked. He *had* been stalking her. Despite the risk of her mother finding out, she needed to immediately call the sheriff on her satellite phone.

Ruger heard a loud shout coming from the north, near Alyna's campsite. He was already halfway there, but now he picked up the pace. A few minutes later, he broke through the tree line into the clearing.

"Argh!" Alyna stood over a pile of junk in front of her tent opening.

Alyna spun around, wielding the pick like a tomahawk she was ready to throw. Her eyes were locked on to the rifle in his right hand. He lowered the weapon and took a step closer. "Are you okay?"

At his question, her gaze flew to meet his. "Am I okay? Did you really just ask me that? Stop attacking me in the middle of the night, stop destroying my stuff, and then I might be okay."

"You know I didn't attack you. I only wanted—"

"The box. Yes, I know. Are you going to kill me for it?"

She meant the gun. He sidestepped over to the edge of her tent and placed the rifle gently on the ground. "Of course not. I'm sorry I took your weapon. I just didn't want you to use it on me." He gave her what he hoped was a charming smile. His gaze fell to the box cradled against her chest like a fussy baby. She clutched it tighter. "Please..." He circled back around, putting some space between him and the gun. "I just need to know what's in there."

A scowl darkened her deep blue eyes. "You mean you don't know? I thought it belonged to you."

The sarcasm dripping out of her lovely lips almost made him laugh. This woman might look too gorgeous to be out here, but she was clearly tough enough. Maybe he should appeal to her emotional side instead of confronting her head-on. "I'm begging you. The box belongs to my family. Please give it to me."

He took several slow steps toward her. She retreated until she was trapped by the tents behind her. He reached a hand out. She stared at it as if it were a snake. Then he realized she was staring at his scar. The flesh torn from his thumb to his wrist had turned thick and white with time. A memento he'd received at ten-years-old from his brother for daring to snoop in his room.

No need to frighten her more than necessary. He reached out with the other hand. The woman stabbed at it with the pick, grazing his knuckles and threatening to give him a matching scar on his left hand. "Would you stop doing that? I'm not going to hurt you."

Her nostrils flared like those of a cornered animal. Such a

betrayal, him forcing her to give it up. But he had no other way to find out what Jared had done. And this stubborn woman wouldn't budge. "Yeah, tell that to my car."

He shrugged. "I don't have much faith in law enforcement, especially not the sheriff in this county. I promise to fix your car later."

As he advanced, he towered over her by at least a foot. She hadn't seemed so short lying in her tent last night. The memory of her peaceful face as she slept, her skin set aglow by moonlight, knocked him back a step. He struggled to focus. She held the pick between them again, using it to point at the mess of junk on the ground. "And how exactly are you going to fix my sat phone?"

Those shattered pieces of metal were from her sat phone? Chills spiraled up his arms, through his shoulders and down his back. He hadn't touched it, hadn't even known she had one. That meant he was running out of time.

He looked up to see Alyna had dropped the rock pick and grabbed the gun in both hands. She pointed it at him, her finger on the trigger. The box lay on the ground behind her feet. *Great. Now what, Lord?*

He peered deep into her cobalt eyes. They were narrowed in anger, but not hardened. Again, he was filled with the certainty she wouldn't shoot him. He stepped closer. Her hand shook on the barrel, but her finger never left the trigger. When his chest was mere inches away from the barrel, he stopped.

Her gaze jumped back and forth from his chest to his eyes. He dipped his head to catch her gaze. Her desperate eyes locked on to his with the force of a tractor beam, and he found he couldn't look away. Her lower lip trembled.

He had to fist his hands to keep from reaching up to touch her face. This was no time to have a physical reaction to a woman. While she was still gazing into his eyes, he grabbed the barrel of the gun and twisted the rifle upward. In a flash, her finger slid off the trigger, and he snagged the butt end out of her hand.

A gasp escaped from her lips. "How did you do that?"

He frowned as heaviness clogged his heart. "I learned a few things in prison."

Her eyes went wide. He could only imagine what she thought about him now. "I'm sorry, but right now it's not safe for you to have this." He bent down and picked up the box.

She moved to stop him, but he pressed the gun into her side, and she froze. Surely she thought he would shoot her. Holding the box in one hand and the gun in the other, he backed away until he reached the edge of the trees. She stood staring at him, anger and betrayal evident in her pinched eyebrows and her clamped mouth. "Why?"

"Because I didn't smash your phone. Which means it had to be my brother."

He leaned down, touched the rifle to the ground and slid it toward her. She might need it for protection, after all. Then he ran into the woods, hugging his prize tight.

FIVE

Prison? What kind of man had she just challenged? Ruger's muscled arms and wide chest, visible through his tight long-sleeved shirt, obviously made him powerful. But did they make him dangerous? He could have killed her today, but he didn't. Instead, his intense gaze had lingered too long on her lips, making her smolder from the inside out. He'd looked more likely to kiss her than shoot her.

Whatever he might think of her, he wanted the box more. But why? Even he didn't seem to know. But it had something to do with his brother.

She thought back to the moment he'd held her gaze. It had contained more than just the fleeting spark of passion. She'd felt a flash of recognition as well. He resembled someone she went to school with, someone a few grades older, although she couldn't recall the name. Could it have been Ruger?

It didn't matter. He'd taken the gemstones found on her claim. Gemstones that could fund her for an entire research season. It was theft, pure and simple. Since she couldn't call in the sheriff, and town was a rugged ten-mile walk through the mountains, she'd have to get her property back on her own. Determination set her jaw. It was time to do a little stalking herself. She picked up the rifle. She'd spent enough time in the wilderness to know how to follow a trail without being heard.

Stepping gingerly into the woods where he'd disappeared, she searched the ground, spying a large footprint next to a broken tree branch, and then another. He'd gone south. She followed the signs of his movement easily for a hundred yards before coming to a small creek. She splashed through the water to the other side. One muddy footprint pointed her to the southwest, but then the trail became harder to find. Ruger had apparently stopped running after crossing the creek.

She paced through the forest, searching for signs of him. At last, she caught sight of a round depression in the soft earth. It looked like a knee-print. Perhaps he had bent down to retie his boots. She walked slowly, all the while looking up at a small hill nearby. Could he have doubled back to a campsite up there? It was what she would do. If so, he could be watching her now.

She stopped, uncertain which way to go. Keep following the tracks or explore the hill? *Lord, what should I do?*

The distant sound of voices filtered through the trees. That had to be her answer. She bent low and crept in that direction. The muffled noises rose and fell in an indistinguishable mass. Still, she kept moving silently. Her thighs burned from moving forward for too many minutes in a crouch, but she couldn't stand if she wanted to get close undetected. She kept her eyes on the ground to avoid stepping on leaves or sticks that might break.

As she approached, the voices became distinct, like someone had turned a radio dial to a new channel. She gripped the rifle tighter, but it no longer made her feel secure. Hunching down behind a thick bush, she gently parted the branches at the bottom. Half-hidden in the trees, a tall, sandy-haired man stood near Ruger. Their faces looked similar—same chin with a slight cleft, same straight nose and strong jaw—but the other man was taller with a shade darker hair, and he carried himself differently, wider somehow. Could this be the brother Ruger had mentioned?

"I knew you wouldn't disappoint me." The man glanced down at the box Ruger still held against his chest.

Ruger didn't answer. He just stared with raised eyebrows and a hint of confusion in his eyes—or was it fear?

"Funny thing, though. You've been out...what has it been...for three months, and you're just now getting over here. Strange because I asked you to come right away." The man took a step closer to Ruger, circling around until his back was to Alyna. His deep voice was menacing. "Or maybe you weren't going to do it at all."

Ruger's Adam's apple bobbed. "I came to do it now. Isn't that enough?" He backed up a step, still clutching the box. "I'll take care of this for you. I'll find a deep lake to drop it in. Let me do this."

Alyna bit her bottom lip. Ruger was a terrible liar.

"Have you looked inside yet?" the man asked.

Ruger shook his head.

"Well, someone has, but you might as well go ahead. Look."

Ruger shifted the box to horizontal and opened the lid. As his eyes took in the gemstones, they widened. His jaw tightened, the muscles pulsing. Did he understand their value? His gaze flipped back to the other man, accusation narrowing his eyes. "For this? Why?"

Heart-wrenching agony scratched through Ruger's voice and stretched the muscles on his face. Those stones meant something more to him than the value they would bring as collector's pieces. But what?

She glanced over at the other man's back. Tingles of alarm ran down her spine. He had reached behind his back and lifted his shirt. The butt of a gun was wedged into the waistband of his jeans. The man wrapped his hand tight around it. Ruger continued to stare at him, oblivious to the threat.

Taking a step closer to Ruger, the man lowered his voice. "Give it to me now."

Ruger shook his head with the defiant expression of a little boy. "You wanted me to see this."

"Actually, I asked you to get rid of it without looking inside. Remember?" The man tugged the gun out and held it flush against his lower back. Ruger still couldn't see it. Alyna had to do something or this guy might really shoot Ruger right in front of her. As quietly as she could, she pushed the barrel of the rifle through the bush. Her hand trembled as she took aim. Could she really shoot someone in the back?

The man's posture shifted a bit. Maybe he'd had a change of heart. "I trusted you to take care of this."

Ruger's dark eyes grew darker as he scrunched his eyebrows together. "Don't make this about us. This is about her."

Her? Who was he talking about?

Ruger held the box up in the air. The stones clacked against each other. She winced at the damage he was likely causing to the specimens, then chided herself for caring. This guy was about to pull out a gun. She crept deeper into the bush, thorns pulling at her sleeves, to get a better sight line.

"What did you even know about her? You were a child." Before Ruger could answer, the man whipped the gun from behind his back. But rather than point it at Ruger, the man slammed the butt into Ruger's head.

As Ruger fell, the man caught the box. Alyna's trigger finger tensed, but still she hesitated. Perhaps he had what he wanted and she didn't need to intervene after all. She held her breath a beat, waiting for the man to leave.

He paced in a small circle, every once in a while glancing down at Ruger's face. A myriad of emotions played across the man's expressive features. The pinch of disappointment, the wide eyes of longing, and finally the scowl of anger.

The man stepped to the side and angled the gun at the back of Ruger's head. The gun shook with his trembling hand. He didn't want to kill Ruger, but he looked ready to do it. She had to stop him. Mentally she willed her trigger finger to contract, to shoot, but her body refused to complete the deed.

"No!" The deep voice came from behind the man.

The man tilted his head as if recognizing the voice, but he didn't respond. Instead, he shoved the gun in the back of his jeans and ran off in the opposite direction.

From the cover of the foliage stepped another man, this one older, his dark hair graying at the temples. He wore a green flannel shirt and jeans, just like the claim jumper she'd spied with the binoculars. Whoever he was, the man with the gun hadn't wanted a confrontation with the claim jumper.

For a few seconds, the claim jumper leaned over Ruger's fallen body, then he disappeared into the same overgrown patch of forest he'd come from.

As soon as both men left, Alyna dashed over to Ruger, surprised at her sudden protectiveness for a man who had broken into her tent and stolen from her. But no matter what Ruger had done, his desperation hadn't scared her as much as the coldness she'd seen on the other man's face once he'd decided to shoot. He'd been all confusion one minute and hard as a rock the next.

She crouched next to Ruger, uncertain what to do. His light hair draped his forehead, disguising the area where he'd gotten hit. She reached up to brush it away, but hesitated. Ruger might be the lesser of two evils here, but there was a good chance he was still dangerous. Even so, given the conversation with that strange man, something more was obviously going on. She'd never get the gemstones back if she didn't stick around long enough to find out what.

As she whisked away his soft hair, her fingers grazed a lump on his forehead. He gasped and blinked, then bolted upright, causing her to backpedal away and land on her rear end. A groan escaped from his lips. "Is he still here?"

"No." He winced at her voice, so she softened it. "Who was that?"

"Are you okay?" he whispered.

Weird that he kept asking her that in these situations. "Me? I'm not the one with a massive lump coming out of my head."

He tried to nod, then seemed to think better of it.

"I gather that was the brother you mentioned."

"Yeah. That's Jared."

She crossed her legs in front of her. "Why did he want the box?"

A long sigh followed by a painful grimace. "They're proof."

"Proof of what?"

Ruger pressed his lips together, as if sealing them would keep her questions at bay.

She wasn't that easily deterred. "What were you going to do with the box?"

"Use it to trap Jared."

She shifted the rifle closer. "Why?"

"I need him to admit what he's done."

A lump formed in the pit of her stomach. "And what's that?"

Rather than answer, Ruger closed his hand around hers. It felt like an apology, and his touch sent a warm rush of tingles racing down her spine. For the first time, she paused to really look at him. His short blond hair was highlighted with a hint of red, as was his nose from a light sunburn. His chocolate-colored brown eyes held her gaze steady, frown wrinkles deepening their depths. This man might have regrets for whatever had sent him to prison, but he wasn't filled with shame. Sitting across from her on the ground, he didn't look nearly as intimidating as when his body had filled up her small tent.

"Okay. How about you fix my car, and I go get the sheriff. Jared attacked you, so you can press charges. He'll go back to jail. Problem solved."

Ruger dropped her hand. The change in temperature left it ice-cold. "No."

"Why not?

In slow, short bursts, he swung his legs around, lifted onto his knees, then stood. He reached down to help her up, but she didn't think he could handle the strain. Instead, she pushed to her feet on her own and held the rifle at her hip. Since he wasn't explaining any of this maybe she should just walk the ten miles to town. But all she really wanted to do was get back the gems Jared had just taken. If that wasn't possible, then she needed to frantically work the claim to replace them. The chill in the air reminded her that she had so few days of good weather left. "Fine. Why should I even care? I'll see you around."

As she turned away, he grabbed her and twisted her back to face him. "I'm sorry, you can't leave."

His brow crinkled. He actually looked sorry, but she didn't care. "What do you mean 'can't'?"

Before she could make a move, Ruger snatched the rifle from her hand. "I need to stop him. Without the police."

He didn't point the gun at her, but the implication was the same. Her blood boiled in her veins, burning off any empathy she might have felt for him. "What are you going to do? He's probably destroying whatever is important in there right now."

A shadow crossed his face. "Maybe, which means I've got to find him and stop him."

She took a step away from him. "You don't need me."

He hefted the gun as if testing its weight. A subtle warning? "No, but I can't let you go..." A short pause. "Until this is over."

Her chest tightened at the determination written in his expression. He'd really kidnap her to get what he wanted. Then, she'd never get enough money to go to Italy this winter. She'd studied for four long years to be able to complete this research for her dad. Now, it all hinged on one unhinged ex-con.

But what could she do? An idea wiggled its way into her head, floating on waves of adrenaline. "What if there was more in the box than gemstones? It might be the proof you need, and you wouldn't have to go after Jared."

His eyes opened wide, and the worry swept off his face. "How?"

"Would you let me go then?"

He tilted his head. "Maybe, depends on what it is."

A glance at the rifle reminded her that she wasn't exactly in the position to bargain for more. She dug into her pocket and held the jump drive out for Ruger to take. Not that she had a choice, but getting involved in this feud between brothers was the worst thing she'd ever done. If Ruger was right, then Jared had some sort of awful secret. And if Ruger was wrong, then the two of them might just kill each other trying to figure it out.

Ruger flipped the drive around in his palm. "This was in the box?"

"At first, I thought it was a map showing the location of the gemstones, but I suppose it could have what you need to prove..." She let the silence linger to punctuate the fact he hadn't told her anything. "Whatever."

"Have you seen the files on here?"

"No, it's password-protected." She inclined her head toward him. "So you'll let me go?"

The ashamed look in his eye gave her the answer. Without knowing what was on there, the drive wasn't enough. He wouldn't let her go.

SIX

As Alyna dutifully trudged through the forest behind Ruger, she wondered if she could jump on him and wrestle the gun away. His arms swung by his sides, the muscles powerful and bulky, one huge fist circling the rifle. She wouldn't have a chance. Right now, he didn't want to hurt her, so she'd count her blessings.

He held the jump drive up between two fingers, peering at it for several minutes as he walked.

"Any idea what might be on there?" At her question, Ruger turned his head. His face was twisted in emotional pain, and she immediately regretted asking. Whatever Jared had done, it was bad. "You know, the sheriff could actually find out what's on that for you."

"No." Ruger turned back around.

That was it. Not only case closed, but locked down without discussion. "Fine, master, sir. Anything else you want me to blindly accept?" What was wrong with her? This man had a gun. She shouldn't be getting sarcastic, but something about him made her want to push. He was a complete contradiction

—rock-hard on the outside, a mess on the inside. It wasn't a stable combination and definitely not someone she should poke at.

He blew out a long sigh. "We can't take it to the sheriff."

She gave him a glare that could have withered the healthiest fireweed flower. Too bad he didn't turn around to see it. "There is no *we*. I don't want to be here, and as soon as you're not looking, I'm gone. But where the sheriff is concerned, you still haven't told me why not."

His voice dropped to little-boy small. "Cops don't always do the right thing."

So much more underlay that statement, but would he tell her? He picked up his pace, suddenly moving with anxious energy. Maybe she could push just a little more. "Jared was going to shoot you."

Ruger stopped walking, keeping his back to her for several moments. When he turned, his face registered sadness, but not the shock she'd expected. "Did you scare him away somehow?"

"No, there was another man. I've never seen him before. The man yelled, then Jared ran." She took a quick breath before continuing. "Don't you see, you can't confront Jared by yourself. You need the police."

Shifting his eyes to the ground, Ruger turned and started walking. She hung back. He seemed preoccupied. Maybe she could slip away. A few feet from her, he twisted at the waist and gestured toward her with the gun, motioning for her to follow.

"Where are we going?" she asked as she matched his pace.

"I've got a campsite about a mile away. No tent, but a sleeping bag with extra blankets."

She shook her head and thrust her hands on her hips. "No way."

Over his shoulder, his smile was weak. "I'll take the blankets and you can have the sleeping bag."

"Instead, let's go back to my campsite first to get my sleeping bag." Then maybe she could find something to help her get away.

His mouth set in a firm line before he turned away from her. "No, Jared would expect us to show up there. He's bound to realize he doesn't have everything in the box."

Us? Again, he'd grouped them together. He must be hoping for a partner, someone to understand his struggle. If she could get him to talk, maybe she could figure out what this was all about. She took on the high-pitched tone of a meddlesome busybody. "Let's see, where did your problems with authority start? Did a guard do something to you in prison? Maybe a fight they wouldn't break up? Or somebody tried to shank you while you slept?"

He frowned at her overdone persona. "Not even close."

She tapped one finger on her lower lip. "Must have been bed-wetting as a child, then."

He actually laughed, a low chuckle that rumbled through his chest. His shoulders relaxed. Mom always said she could charm people, despite her introverted ways. "You are definitely the first girl to call me a bedwetter just to get information out of me."

"Aha, I get it. It's about a girl. Some cop stole your girlfriend."

He raised one eyebrow to say *as if.* "This is entertainment for you? You're going to make up stories about me for the rest of our time together?"

The rest of our time? Exactly how long did he plan to keep her? "Well, maybe...unless you give me something to work with."

He glanced back at her, biting his lip, before turning around to walk forward again. She strained to catch the words he threw over his shoulder. "I went to prison because Jared asked me to deliver a package."

Okay, that wasn't where she'd thought he would start, but she wanted the answer to that question as well.

"Jared said it contained documents for a transaction and that his usual courier was out sick. Since I used to be a tax accountant, I had free time during the summer after all my clients had filed, so I had nothing better to do. I should have known when he offered to pay me two hundred dollars for the day, but I thought he was being generous because of my seasonal income." His shoulders tensed again. "At the delivery address, the police were waiting. Not a swarm like in the movies. Just a few cops who forced me to lie on the ground and arrested me. At the police station, the Fort Collins cops told me I'd been carrying sheets and sheets of counterfeit fifty-dollar bills. I had no idea, and the cops knew it. They wanted me to testify against my brother, told me I could walk out the door if I did, but I didn't know anything. Because I was truly innocent, I couldn't help their case, so instead they put me on trial *with* him."

"Would you have testified against him if you could have?"

He shrugged. "I don't know. Probably not."

"You have a track record of covering for him?" It might explain why Jared thought he could get away with all of this.

"No, well, sometimes. You've got to understand. Jared makes all the trouble he causes seem like it's my fault." Ruger shook his head. "But not anymore."

The image of Jared holding the gun over Ruger's head made her shiver. Jared was dangerous and probably capable of anything Ruger suspected. But what about Ruger? Who knew what he was capable of if she didn't do what he wanted.

Her thoughts locked on to the claim jumper. The man obviously didn't want violence since he'd saved Ruger. Maybe he was a Good Samaritan and would help her get out of this somehow.

"Jared was supposed to be in prison for ten years, but his appeal has granted him a new trial. I only found out a few days ago that he was going to be released."

He'd skirted around the issue. Not good enough. "So you explained why you don't like the Fort Collins police, but I know the sheriff and he's from Stone Alley. Why not trust him?"

A quick turn of his head, followed by a pointed look, then a relinquishing sigh. "Sheriff Hank Everett was a close friend of Jared's back in high school."

"That was ten years ago. So what?"

He opened his hand flat, holding the jump drive up almost as though offering it to God. "I'm not taking any chances with this. It's all I have left."

The pained note in his last words squelched her desire to ask more questions. She silently followed the shadowed outline of Ruger in front of her. Darkness draped slowly through the trees like a living thing reaching down to wrap them up in black tentacles. She'd spent the whole summer out here with Quin and had never had this ominous feeling about nightfall. But was Jared or Ruger the one who made her so nervous?

The only man she could completely trust right now was Quin, and he wasn't coming back for two days. Even when he did, he'd have a hard time finding her if she didn't get back to camp.

Just as she thought it might be dark enough to try to slip away, Ruger stopped ahead of her. She swerved to avoid crashing into his back.

"Here we are." He grabbed a jug. "I'll get some water."

She held her breath. Would he really leave her alone?

As he turned his back, he realized his obvious mistake. "You're coming with me."

She walked behind him, wondering what could get her out of this. Maybe the jump drive was full of junk. Then Ruger could go back to living wherever he normally lived and leave her forest. But her computer was back at camp, so she didn't have any way to attempt to break into the drive.

For tonight, she was stuck with him. Hopefully tomorrow she could convince him to return to her camp. She followed him to the river, filled her water bottle, and trekked behind back to his campsite.

Once there, he unrolled his sleeping bag, then spread the blankets on the ground a few feet away. *Good.* They would definitely not be sleeping together.

After he finished, he swept a hand toward the sleeping bag and offered her a granola bar from his backpack. She gratefully accepted and bit into it as she lowered herself onto the sleeping bag. Her head still buzzed with questions, but before she could ask anything, Ruger spoke.

"Thank you for giving me the jump drive."

The guilt lacing through his voice made her think he would have taken it if he would've known she had it. She kept a close eye on the gun that he placed at the head of the blanket pile before he sat down.

"My mom was a prospector like you, although it was more of a hobby." He scooted the blankets a bit closer. "What made you decide to do it for a living?"

Moonlight filtered through the trees and reflected off the short spikes of his hair, the milky light surrounding him almost like a halo. But despite his angelic appearance, she hesitated to answer him. He'd probably think she was just as nuts as her mom did. But if she opened up a little, he might return the favor. "Actually, I'm prospecting to fund archeological research." She still couldn't seem to call it *her* research. It would always belong to her father. "This autumn, if I can get the funds, I'll travel to Italy for a dig."

"Really? What time period do you specialize in?"

And this was the part where he might think her crazy. But why should she care? He couldn't exactly judge her. He was a kidnapper. "I'll be looking in the basement of an ancient church for Veronica's Veil." Not the same church her father had died in, but still her stomach tightened into knots.

Ruger had lifted the canteen to his lips for a drink, and now he coughed out a little water. "You mean from the Bible?"

Her eyes widened. *He read the Bible?* "That's the one. Veronica, although that was probably not her real name, met Jesus on the way to His crucifixion and gave Him a cloth to wipe His face. His image is supposed to be burned into the garment." She didn't mention it had reportedly been responsible for several acts of divine healing before it was lost sometime around the sacking of Rome. No need to seem like a total nutcase.

"Smart *and* brave. I'm impressed."

She blinked and peered through the dark. His head was tilted down, so she couldn't see his eyes, but she didn't detect any mocking in his tone. "Most people tell me how ridiculous it is to search for a myth." Even her mom, a devout Christian, didn't believe in the relic, hence the major conflict in their marriage. It rubbed her raw when Dad decided to make the veil the focus of his research.

"I can see why people would think so. It sounds pretty dramatic."

Interesting word. Although she was usually opposed to drama, she could live with that description. At least he didn't think she was crazy to search for something she couldn't prove existed. And he didn't even know the real reason why she was looking.

Ruger turned to face her more and the outline of his chiseled features came into focus. "Until prison, I'd never read the Bible. I guess I would have said I believed in God, but I didn't know who He was. On my first day inside, I sat too close to another inmate and was beaten up pretty badly. I ended up in the infirmary, where the Bible is standard issue." He chuckled ruefully. "I suppose they figure you need it. Once I started reading, I couldn't stop. It was my lifeline in there." He lay on his side and shifted a blanket under his head as a pillow. "I remember the story of a woman on the road to Calvary. It could be real."

Her kidnapper was a Christian. *Seriously? Lord, is this Your idea of a joke?* She searched her brain, but couldn't remember *Thou Shalt Not Kidnap* being in the Bible, although this could certainly fit in the *Do Unto Others as You Would Have Them Do Unto You* category. She pushed all those objections down because he seemed actually interested. No one besides Quin had been open-minded enough to consider the veil's existence. "The veil isn't a quest that I started. It meant so much to my father that it feels right to keep searching for it."

Ruger nodded as though he understood. It was surreal, talking to him like a normal person right after he'd kidnapped her. Maybe it was Stockholm syndrome.

He rubbed his hands on his jeans. "Your dad is gone?"

Nodding, she swallowed back a lump. Four years wasn't long enough to cool the heat of grief inside her. "He died at a dig site. A tunnel in the basement of a church collapsed on him."

"I'm so sorry. He didn't deserve that."

The truth of his words zipped straight to the molten place inside her, striking it like a lightning bolt. Her father hadn't deserved it, but her mother had always said he wouldn't have been there if he'd given up the veil like she'd told him to. She'd implied it was his fault, making Alyna defend him.

For Ruger to know just what to say, he must have had experience with loss. But Alyna was too fragile right now to ask him about it. Instead, she blurted, "What are you going to do with the jump drive?"

He went quiet for several minutes. Then, his head popped up and the whites of his eyes shone in the dark as his eyes went wide. "You're good at traps."

Uh-oh. She didn't like where this was going. "Why don't you just take the jump drive to the state police instead of the sheriff?"

"They don't have jurisdiction. Besides, we don't even know if there's anything incriminating on here. This is our one chance—" He cleared his throat. "*My* one chance to trap him and get the rest of the evidence he took. Maybe even get a confession." His eyes drooped at the corners, pleading with her. In other circumstances she would have thought he was adorable in a sad-puppy kind of way. "You could rig something up, right?"

"Why should I help you?"

His eyes hardened, and he motioned to the gun on the ground. "You don't really have a choice."

How quickly he morphed from concern over her grief to threatening her. And he appeared just as sincere on both accounts. Prison had likely taught him the trick of efficiently switching his emotions on and off.

He turned on a placating tone. "You'll get back to your mining claim quicker if you help."

Ugh. He knew just where to push her. Sucking in a deep breath, she conceded, at least in her mind, that he had a point. Once Jared realized the jump drive was missing, he would keep coming after it. Which left them sitting ducks, waiting for him to strike. Unless she caught him first.

SEVEN

Ruger woke as the first rays of a milky dawn broke through the canopy of trees. Most of his body was still cocooned inside the two blankets, but his arm—*whoa*—his arm had stretched out to Alyna, and his hand rested on the back of her shoulder. Quickly, he pulled back the traitorous limb. She'd probably punch him if she woke up to feel his hand on her.

She rolled over, her sleeping face landing just inches from his. With her hands tucked under her chin and her cheeks pink from the cool night air, she looked like an auburn-haired china doll. A thin breath of air drifted from her lips, soft pink and partly open. What would running his thumb along her lower lip feel like? Desire swelled in his gut, and he averted his eyes. She would surely shut down any interest he might have. He was under no illusions of what he was now. An ex-con. Not the kind of guy a woman brought home to her parents.

He rolled onto his back and stared up into the canopy of leaves. A twitch started under his left eye. He'd already put his whole future at risk, and it hadn't seemed as dangerous until Alyna got involved. Kidnapping her could put him back in prison for the rest of his life. Even so, according to what Alyna had said, he should be more focused on keeping them alive. He had no doubt Jared would have pulled the trigger if the other man hadn't stopped him. Who was he? Ruger had his suspicions, but he didn't want to believe it.

A groan came from Alyna. He glanced over to see her brow wrinkled. A nightmare he caused by giving her all this stress? If she helped him capture Jared, he'd let her go immediately. Maybe he could convince her not to press charges after she knew what Jared had done.

Movement had him looking at her again. She sat up, giving him a dazed stare. She ran a hand through her mass of hair, tugging at the strands to straighten them. He smiled at her attempts to get herself together. As if prim and proper could be any more attractive than her innocent, rumpled morning look. "Don't worry, nature looks good on you." He meant it literally as he picked a stray stick out of her hair.

She grunted.

Her surly response only increased his need to tease her. "It might be because of the movie *Tomb Raider*, but I've always had a thing for archeologists." A small voice in his head yelled at him to stop flirting. She would never be interested, but he didn't want to stop. The heated blush rising on her cheeks was enough to keep him going. "Or maybe I just never grew up, and I like a girl who's willing to play in the dirt."

She swallowed hard, then broke eye contact. "My mom would be horrified to hear you encouraging me to play in the dirt."

"Why?"

"She never wanted me to emulate my dad. She thinks archeology ruined his life. Considering what happened, I can't really argue the point."

"Then why do you follow in his footsteps?" The instant pinch of emotional pain on her face shocked him. He'd been insensitive. During his time in prison, he'd forgotten how to talk to women. But before he could apologize, lightning-fast, the pain was gone. Her expression was now placid and detached.

"I studied archeology so I could finish his work. His life meant something. I mean, I have to make sure it did."

A cryptic answer. "Is there something else you'd rather do?"

He got to his feet, looking down at her. She didn't meet his gaze, and her lips were planted in a thin line, anxiety wrinkling the edges of her mouth.

He shrugged. "Fine, don't tell me."

Again, her stressed-out demeanor gradually faded to a calm, emotionless expression. When she met his gaze, her face was stoic. "What I want to do doesn't seem like the right thing to do, so I'm doing this for my father. Does that make sense?"

Oddly, it did. She'd chosen archeology for him and now she didn't know how to go back on that. He knew from experience that the memory of a loved one was a powerful motivator. "But what would you do if you could choose with no strings attached?"

A dark cloud passed overhead, shadowing her face. He couldn't see her reaction, but her silence spoke volumes.

"You don't have to tell me. But trust me, you should figure out what you love and do that. Don't waste time. Don't waste your freedom." He hadn't meant them to sound ominous, but his stern words seemed to echo off the trees.

Her dark eyebrows dipped. "Believe me, I'm extremely conscious of my lack of freedom."

He gulped. "I deserved that. All right, let's get this done. Any ideas for a trap?"

A devious gleam brightened her eyes. "Actually, yes, but I'll need some supplies from town."

Ruger shook his head. "I can't let you go."

"Then you'll just have to come with me." She ignored him as

though the matter was already decided while she tugged a hair band off her wrist and swept her gorgeous auburn strands into a long ponytail. At least that would make it easier to stave off the desire to run his hands through it.

She caught him staring and a light blush crept up her neck. "We have to take the risk if you want to catch him." She stomped a foot. "And we are going to catch him alive."

He frowned, resenting the implication he wanted Jared caught dead or alive. "Fine, but we need to be cautious." He'd already disrupted Alyna's life by forcing her to stay, no way to change that, but if they had to go into town, he had to keep control of her.

"By the way, do you have any food?" she asked.

He offered her a granola bar. "Just these."

"Nothing else?"

He shook his head.

She ripped open the bar and took a bite. "I have some dehydrated meals in a tree stash near my car."

They hiked in silence to within a few hundred yards of her car. She pointed out the tree where a large plastic box hung. He cut the rope to retrieve it. Inside, he found a dozen meals of dried fruit, meat and vegetables. He put them in his backpack, and they kept walking.

At her campsite, Alyna grabbed a backpack and pulled her keys from it. They walked down to her car where she popped open the trunk. "Let me see what I have."

Rummaging through duffel bags, she began tossing seemingly random metal parts on the ground as she grunted and mumbled to herself, not sounding happy with the search.

"So what's your idea?" he asked.

"A modified version of a conibear trap. That's a type of body-gripping trap."

Yeah, like that explained everything.

She looked up at the tree canopy and huffed, blowing stray hairs off her forehead. "Why can't I find it?"

"What?"

"The CO2 cartridge." She answered without looking at him, her head back in the trunk searching for the canister. "Oh, here it is. But..."

Ruger peered over her shoulder. The cartridge in her hand was mangled and the end had popped off. Obviously something had fallen on it, expelling all the gas.

A moment of silence ticked by as Alyna tapped a finger on her lower lip. "The hardware store should have another one, along with the metal jaws. Time to go into town."

"I don't know." What if he lost control of her? What if they ran into Jared?

She came close, positioning her body inches away, and looked up at him. Her sapphire-blue eyes blinked a few times. He gazed down at her upturned face, acutely aware of how tiny she was compared to him. She tilted her head and her ponytail swayed over her shoulder. All his senses, every nerve, buzzed with electricity. He knew she was working him, but he didn't care as long as she stayed close. "You need the CO2 and the other metal thing?"

She nodded. "The trap won't work without them."

She didn't beg to leave, but she pleaded with her eyes—and she was doing a pretty good job of it. He swallowed hard, then turned his gaze to the trees beyond her. She seemed sincere about needing to go, but he still didn't know if he could trust her. Would she scream bloody murder the second other people were around? Then again, she was the one who had reason not to trust him. "You promise you won't try to escape?"

She hesitated, but answered firmly. "I promise."

Satisfied she meant it, he walked to a nearby tree where he'd hidden her spark plugs. "I'll put these back in."

Within minutes, he sat next to her as she drove down the mountain road. Last night, he'd heard Alyna praying just before she fell asleep. All he could do now was trust that as a Christian she wouldn't break her promise. But after the number of times Jared had betrayed him, trust felt foreign.

As they neared the highway, Alyna glanced at him from the corner of her eye. "You must have some idea what's on the jump drive."

The woman was relentless. Ruger rubbed at his temples. He could blow her off again, but he kind of owed her for getting her involved.

Tell her. The quiet voice inside his head was insistent. He took a deep breath. "Just before I left prison, Jared asked me to find something and get rid of it."

"The box."

He gently nodded, trying not to exacerbate his headache. "I've always done what he asked. But this was different." He shifted to hold his head at the temples, eyes staring at the floor of the car. "His cellmate had mentioned a month before that Jared was claiming credit for a murder. Guys do that in prison, so I didn't worry about it much. Until Jared asked me to cover something up. So I went back to Jared's cellmate to find out who Jared had confessed to killing." Ruger's breath hitched, the familiar tremor racking his chest. This part was the hardest to believe, yet now he knew it had to be true. "It was my mother...our mother."

Alyna sat straight up, gripping the wheel with knuckles that were turning white, but he couldn't bring himself to look at her face.

His eyes burned, but he pushed back the tears. "When I was thirteen, my mother suddenly disappeared. The gems in the box were ones she'd collected on her prospecting trips." He jammed his hands into his lap. "Getting Jared to admit what he did is the only way to find my mom."

Alyna stayed silent. After a few minutes, Ruger sneaked a glance her way. Her jaw twitched and her shoulders were stiff. Did she feel any compassion for him? Or was she still just as angry about the situation?

As they pulled into Stone Alley, he hadn't gotten any clue as to whether she would behave. She parked in front of Schroeder's Hardware store, and they got out of the car. Down the street, near Mary's Cafe, the overhead lights of a police cruiser stuck up above the row of cars. Probably the sheriff. The tremor in his chest turned into an earthquake.

As casually as possible, he slung the rifle over his shoulder and walked toward the door. *That's right, just a hunter making a quick stop before going into the mountains.*

No one on the street paid them any attention. He pulled open the door and stepped into the oddly comforting smell of wood and grease.

"Not in here." The man at the counter pointed at the rifle, barely looking up from the computer screen. "Leave it by the door."

Ruger dropped the weapon on a bench, turning his body away from the man. Ruger hadn't been inside the store in years, but people in small towns were notorious for remembering folks. If he remembered correctly himself, the man at the counter was Adam Schroeder, the owner. A short, thin man in his lower forties, Adam had a brightness to his eyes that made him seem younger. Thankfully, Adam turned away to address another customer, telling the man he could order the saw blade he wanted.

Ruger bent down to whisper in Alyna's ear. "Don't say anything to him about me or Jared. I don't want to hurt anyone, but I will if I have to." He screwed up his eyebrows, hoping he looked fierce, hoping she'd buy it.

With a nod, she took the lead, ducking into the nearest

aisle. He followed, staying on the left side of the aisle to angle his body out of Adam's view. Screwdrivers and hammers covered the shelves. Not likely the things she would need for the trap, but hopefully she knew her way around here better than he did.

He hung close to her heels as she quickly wove through the aisles to the power tools.

"Finding what you need, Alyna?"

Adam's gruff voice startled them. With no time to shoot her a warning glare, Ruger pasted on his most innocent face and turned around. Maybe he'd be able to fade into the background while Alyna talked to Adam.

No such luck. Adam directed his words to Alyna, but his gaze was fixed on Ruger. "Everything okay?"

Alyna flipped her ponytail over her shoulder. Was she trying to be casual or was it nerves? "Sure. I've got one thing I need." She grabbed a CO_2 cartridge, then grabbed another one. "But I also need a conibear trap." She snapped her fingers. "And some more explosives."

"Uh, huh." Adam still didn't take his eyes off Ruger. "Who's this?"

"Just a friend." A nervous pause. "He's helping me while Quin is hanging out at home for the weekend." Even to Ruger it sounded contrived. Wait a minute? Who was Quin?

"I'm not sure your boyfriend would approve."

Quin had to be her boyfriend. A sharp pang twisted in his stomach and it had nothing to do with them getting caught. He barely knew this woman, but the thought of her being off the market disappointed him.

Alyna gave Adam a scorching look, drawing his attention. He put his hands up in surrender. "Okay. Sorry, but I can't help you with the trap or the explosives. My last trap went to Mr. Johnson for his hunting trip, and oddly enough, I had a break-in last night.

Somebody stole my entire supply of gunpowder and some ammo."

"That's awful."

"Yeah, the sheriff is looking into it. Just when you think an area is safe." He folded his arms across his chest. "Speaking of risky, when are you going to give up this crazy idea of being a prospector?"

Fire flashed in her eyes. "You're saying that because I'm a woman."

"Well, yes...and no. Prospecting is dangerous for anyone. It's not worth the risk."

"It is if you love it." The answer was so quiet, Ruger almost missed it. Her eyes went wide as though she couldn't believe she'd said it out loud.

Adam slowly nodded, but his frown said he was still disappointed in her answer. With one finger, he indicated the cartridges. "Are you ready, then?"

"Maybe. Give me a second to think about a workaround."

Switching his gaze back to Ruger, Adam backed away. "When you're ready, I'll ring you up at the counter."

A massive torrent of confusion raged in Ruger's stomach. He couldn't decide if he was more miserable over Alyna having a boyfriend or her choice of career. If she loved prospecting, she should be doing that, not chasing after her father's legacy. When he was sure Adam couldn't hear, he whispered, "Why not prospecting?"

She bit her lip for several seconds before speaking in a soft voice. "It's not an appropriate career."

Those words didn't even sound like hers. "Gem hunting isn't good enough for you?"

Her hair draped over one shoulder as she shrugged. "As my mom is always reminding me, I can't help anyone in the middle of nowhere. How do I show God's love to the world from out there?"

Now he understood. Jesus said to point others to Him. Ruger took a step closer to her, staring right into her eyes. He didn't know her well, but he had to tell her what he saw. "Alyna, you're a wanderer, an adventurer, an explorer. Those aren't bad things to be. In fact, they're pretty amazing." He lifted his hand, then chastised himself for wanting to caress her cheek. He dropped his arm. "When God gives you a love for something, you have to pursue it with all of your heart."

She backpedaled a step, surprise furrowing her brow. He realized this was the first time he'd mentioned God to her in a way that wasn't in the past. God was real and present, but since entering the mountains, he hadn't acted like he believed that. A pang of insecurity hit him. Who was he to say anything about God's plans? Ruger had no idea where his own life was going.

A flash of dark gray caught his eye. "Oh no. Stay quiet." He grabbed her shoulders and swung her down the next aisle just as the sheriff passed where they had been standing. Had he seen them?

She barely had time to register a large chest with a badge pinned to it before Ruger had shifted them both away. The sheriff. The sensible thing to do would be to snag his attention. Somehow, her conscience balked at that. Ruger had kidnapped her and threatened her, but he'd also refused to hurt her to get the box and just now, he'd tried to encourage her to follow her heart. He'd done so many things to prove he was a criminal, and yet there was more to him. Could she betray him? Could she betray her own promise? And what would he do if the sheriff cornered him?

Although, she didn't agree with his suspicions of the sheriff from what Ruger had said in the car his motives were pure. No one should be left with the unanswered question of what happened to a loved one.

Ruger peered over her head, his warm hands still on her arms. She looked up at his jawline, the sensitive skin of his neck that smelled like pine and fresh air. She'd better watch herself before this became more than just getting back to her claim. He'd professed to be a Christian, so he owed her a promise in return. "Promise you will let me go after I catch Jared for you."

He looked down at her, his face inches from hers, his eyes deep and dark. "I will."

She nodded, then slipped away from his grasp, much too aware of his strong presence following her. On the way to the register, she grabbed some extra rope and a net from a display shelf. She already had some, but they had to change plans, and Jared was a big man to tie up. At the register, Ruger threw money down for the supplies, then hovered by the door. Not yet touching his gun, but ready to scoop it up and leave.

"Surprised you're not up on the mountain this early." Adam's tone sounded suspicious, but it was hard to tell with his gravelly voice. Typically, she would dig for gems during the morning and early afternoon. If she came to the hardware store, it was normally just before his late afternoon closing time.

"It was a little cool this morning."

His eyes narrowed. "That doesn't usually bother you."

She shrugged. "I don't know. Maybe I'm coming down with something. I've got a bit of a headache." That was the truth at least.

"I don't see how you'd catch anything, what with your *boyfriend* being here in town."

His sarcastic tone grated on her nerves. He meant Quin, but for a second a different picture flashed through her mind. Ruger last night, moonlight highlighting his features, watching her just before she drifted off to sleep. Something was definitely wrong with her head.

Adam bagged her purchases. As she reached to take the bag, he held on to it. "Find anything interesting up there?"

Her gut soured with fear. But he couldn't possibly know. "Like what?"

He lifted his brows in an incredulous expression, effectively saying she was an idiot. "I don't know, maybe gemstones?"

"Oh, sorry. Told you I've got a headache." Good stall, but he kept waiting for her answer. What could she say that wasn't a lie? "A few promising specimens have fallen out of the claim, although I'm not sure I can bring them in yet."

"Nice. Well, if you need any more help..." He lifted an arm and curled his small bicep. She almost laughed, but caught herself just in time, because he was clearly only half-kidding.

"Thanks for the offer, but I've already got more partners than I need."

She swung toward the door and smacked right into a large chest. One wearing a shiny silver badge. Sheriff Hank grabbed her arms. "Are you okay?"

Where is Ruger?

Gulping in a big breath, she lifted her eyes to meet his gaze. His bushy eyebrows were knotted up in concern. "I'm fine. Sorry."

Running into the sheriff on her way out the door seemed too much of a coincidence. Was God trying to tell her to get help? She opened her mouth, then snapped it shut again. Ruger's fear of police was well founded and strong enough to make him want to take on Jared alone. Despite her claim to Ruger that she knew Sheriff Hank, she didn't know anything about his past or whether he'd be loyal to a high school friend. Sheriff Hank smiled at her and stepped up to the counter to pay for his items. She turned away with a stone weighing on her chest. She'd made her choice and somehow ended up on Ruger's side. Maybe Mom was right and all her decisions were questionable.

As she pushed through the door, a deep breath of the cool mountain air and the sight of Ruger waiting by the car eased her tension. It would all go according to her plan, and if Jared had done anything, they would get a confession out of him. At that point, Sheriff Hank wouldn't be able to protect Jared.

"Alyna!"

Her feet froze at the recognizable shout that came from behind. She turned and searched the sidewalk. Her mom ran toward her, waving frantically.

"I thought that was your car." Her mom panted, not used to any type of running.

"Mom, I—"

"I was worried about you. I couldn't get you to answer the satellite phone."

She shrugged an apology. "It's broken."

"How?"

"You know, stuff happens. Did you need something?"

Her mother planted her feet and locked her fists on her hips, a stance that looked all too familiar since Alyna had used it several times on Ruger lately. "I need my daughter to stop working by herself in the middle of nowhere for no good reason." Her voice softened as she touched Alyna's arm. "I worry about you, honey."

"I know, but look at me. I'm safe, healthy, even got a little tan in the last couple of days. You can't ask for more."

"I thought I was going to have to send out a search party."

At least Mom hadn't told the sheriff she wasn't answering or he would have said something in the store.

"Who's that?" Mom's gaze had gone to the car.

Ruger leaned casually against the hood, his back to them.

Thankfully, the rifle was nowhere in sight. "Someone who's helping me while Quin is gone."

"Does he live around here?"

"He used to." Alyna backed away. "I've got to go."

Mom took a step toward her, a suspicious glint in her eyes. "I want to come meet this guy."

Alyna stepped sideways to block her path. "Next time, okay? I really need to get back to the claim."

"Actually, you should get back there. I wasn't the only one worried. Quin went back to the claim early to check on you. He's probably there right now."

"Oh." Alyna covered her horror at the idea of Quin finding the trashed tent and sat phone. He'd be terrified for her. "Right, I've got to go let him know that I'm okay. See you later." She turned away, leaving Mom standing on the sidewalk. Before jumping into her car, she called out one last thing. "And when you get a chance, order me a new sat phone, please. Thanks."

EIGHT

With barely a word to Ruger, Alyna drove as fast as she dared along the winding road back to the campsite. She didn't think he'd heard what her mother said about Quin being up here, and she didn't feel like explaining right now. A hundred yards from camp, she parked behind Quin's vehicle. At least he was still here.

Ruger looked curiously at the car as she pulled up, then asked for her car keys before she bolted from it. He was still keeping tabs on her. She threw them at him and darted into the clearing. It was empty.

She stood there for a second before thinking he might have gone up to the claim. She turned toward the woods, but only made it a few feet. Footsteps were coming her way.

Ruger had come up behind her. His tense shoulders said he'd heard it too. She was suddenly grateful for his protection as he raised the rifle and trained it on the trees.

She pressed her back against the nearest tree trunk, praying it would be big enough to hide her. As the person passed by on her right, she peeked out. "Quin!"

He ran toward her. "Alyna." Her name was a strangled cry. He grabbed her by the arms. "You're okay? What happened? The place looks like a bomb went off. I thought—"

"I'm fine." She'd rather not hear what he'd feared.

He spread his hand out in the direction of camp. "Was it a bear?"

"No, but we have to leave. It's not safe here."

Quin looked up, for the first time noticing Ruger with a rifle aimed at him.

"So this is your boyfriend." Ruger's voice was menacing.

Stepping around her, Quin confronted Ruger. "What's going on?"

Alyna stepped sideways to face Ruger as well. "Quin is my partner. We prospect up here together. He couldn't reach me on the sat phone and came up to see if I was okay."

She detailed the events of the last two days to Quin, only leaving out that Ruger had been in jail and the strange way her heart kicked into overdrive when Ruger came too close. A tiny hiccup in her gut reminded her this strange attraction to Ruger had probably made her biased.

After she finished, Quin remained silent—definitely not normal. He usually had an opinion on everything. She stepped in front of him to force him to look at her. "Say something."

"Fine. This is crazy." His hands gestured wildly. "How could you trust some random guy who shows up out of nowhere?" The hurt in his eyes flashed fire before he reined it back in. "He could be the claim jumper trying to lure you away from our site."

"He's not. I saw the claim jumper. It's an older guy, maybe around sixty."

"Oh, great. There's someone else out here to worry about. But seriously, you don't trust this guy, do you?"

That was the question she'd wrestled with for hours. Her gaze darted to Ruger, but she couldn't read his expression. He kept the gun leveled at waist height, looking impassively at their exchange. She shifted her attention back to Quin and decided to answer honestly. "I don't know. But if your mom disappeared, wouldn't you want to find the truth?" Deep down, she understood Ruger's need for justice. It stemmed from the desire to make a horrible thing somehow turn out right. For there to be a reason, an end, a resolution. It was the same thing she wanted for her father.

Quin's put his hands on her arms and she felt him tremble. She'd never seen him this agitated before. "Other than Ruger's word that the jewels belonged to his mom, you have no proof Jared has done anything."

He had a point. Ruger could have made it up on the way to town to ensure her continued cooperation.

"I know you." Ruger's voice hadn't lost any of its menace.

Quin shook his head. "You don't look familiar."

"From high school." Ruger took several steps closer to Quin, the height difference magnifying with each step. Ruger towered over him by six inches. "You were one of Jared's friends."

Quin looked up at him. "Yeah, I knew him. So what? We had a big group of friends in high school." Rolling his shoulders back, Quin puffed out his chest. "I demand you let her go. Take me instead."

She admired the bravery it took to demand anything from a stranger holding a gun, and Quin's willingness to trade himself for her made her heart swell. He'd been her friend for several years, but they'd only gotten to be close friends on the claim this summer when they'd spent most nights talking about crazy places they wanted to visit or other gems they wanted to mine across the country. But they had never been through something stressful like this, and it was nice to know he wouldn't cut and run.

If Ruger agreed to her release, she'd have another difficult decision on her hands. Go to the sheriff or give them time to trap

Jared first? Part of the reason she hadn't tried to signal the sheriff in town was because she didn't want Ruger to do something stupid, but if he set her free...

"Answer me."

She expected Quin to demand they contact the sheriff next, but he just waited for Ruger to respond. She held her breath, wondering how the stalemate would break, ignoring the niggling question of whether she wanted to stay with Ruger. Right now, she didn't have a choice.

"Fine. You won't even talk. Then we're both leaving." Quin grabbed her arm, propelling her toward his car. They only made it a few steps.

Ruger let out a low growl, lifted the rifle, and spun around.

Quin dragged her to the ground and covered her with his arms. Her head twisted, but she could still see Ruger from the corner of her eye.

He took aim, then fired a shot straight into the grill of Quin's vehicle.

Her mouth dropped open as metal split and flew out from the gaping wound in the vehicle. The noise echoed through the trees, bouncing back to her ears again and again, bringing with it the realization that now Quin didn't have a choice about staying either.

Lowering the weapon, Ruger spoke in a frustrated tone. "You can either stay here and deal with my brother, who I'm sure will investigate the gunshot, or you can come with me." He turned his back and strode into the forest.

When Quin got off her, Alyna snatched up their two sleeping bags and her laptop with its case. Quin stared at his vehicle in confusion. As she darted toward the safety of the trees, she looked over her shoulder. Quin still stood rooted to the ground.

"We really should go," she said.

"I'll walk back to town and get help."

There was the sensible, logical Quin she'd come to depend on. She retraced her steps to stand in front of him. "You don't have a weapon. What if Jared finds you?"

This seemed to give him pause.

"Ruger has my keys. We don't have any way to leave, so I think we're safer as a group." A few seconds later, she added, "For now."

She took a step back, and he followed, grumbling. "Not much safer with a testosterone-driven nutcase like him."

They easily caught up to Ruger. He'd probably been waiting to make sure one of them didn't try to leave. Walking in silence, she felt smashed between two men who couldn't have been any different. Quin, so methodical he'd admitted to color-coding his T-shirt drawer. Ruger, who had charged into the woods to find the box without much of a plan at all. Behind her, Quin fretted and stewed about their situation. Ahead, Ruger held the tension in his shoulders. Come to think of it, the rifle slung across his muscled back gave him a rugged, adventurous look that was nearly irresistible. Or maybe she'd watched too many *Indiana Jones* movies as a kid.

When they reached camp, the sun had dipped more than halfway down the sky. Ruger tossed the hardware store bag on the ground, and Quin gestured at it. "I know how much Alyna loves a good trap, but if we capture Jared for you, then we're done with all this. Right?"

"That's the plan," Alyna answered for Ruger as she sat next to the bag and dug through it. "Except I don't have a metal trap. I'm going to have to rig something up with rope."

"Okay." Quin glared at Ruger while still speaking to her. "Besides, there's no way I'd leave you out here alone with him." He turned back to her, stretching his voice into a low, gravelly bass. "He's like a cast member from *The Godfather*."

Ruger grunted, his knuckles tightening on the rifle. Alyna

stifled a giggle. One of the things she loved about Quin was his unusual sense of humor. But now wasn't the best time for jokes. They had to figure out how to capture a man who would kill them for the jump drive.

A loud explosion rocked the air around them, reverberating off the surrounding mountains. Alyna jumped to her feet. "What was that?"

Ruger had already disappeared into the forest, probably in search of a view from higher ground. She sped after him, quickly surpassing him thanks to her superior climbing ability. At the top of the nearest peak, she broke out of the tree line and scanned the horizon. Ruger came up behind her, and she heard Quin making his way up as well.

She circled around and her eyes snagged on a spot in the distance where smoke drifted up, a dark trail spiraling into the powder-blue sky. Her heart skipped a beat. Without the binoculars she couldn't be sure, but the location seemed suspiciously close to—*no.*

"Jared blew up your claim." Ruger cursed, then quickly began apologizing to the sky.

She narrowed her eyes, peering harder at the peak. It had to be a mistake.

Using the surrounding landmarks, she mentally calculated the spread of the horizon and the angle upslope. The truth hit her like a sledgehammer. Their claim was covered in smoke. As the wind cleared the air, she saw the tall spire had fallen over. From this distance, it looked like a matchstick discarded on the rocky stubble of the mountainside.

Her pulse jumped up in her throat. The claim was gone. All the stunning gemstones—her only way to pay for her father's research—were demolished. And she was supposed to leave in a month. A prickle of tears burned her eyes. "Why would he do that?"

Ruger let out a long sigh. He waited so long to say something that she thought about shaking his shoulders, but if she started yelling, the tears would flow. When he finally spoke, his voice was hard. "He's sending us a message."

Quin growled, "That's a lot of bang for one message."

"He wants me—" Ruger turned to Alyna, piercing her with his dark eyes. "*Us* to know he's coming for the jump drive."

For the first time, she didn't argue about there being an us. This unstable alliance had already cost her too much. And if Jared found them, it could cost much more.

NINE

The next morning broke with a dusty covering of clouds. Alyna rolled over and struggled to wake. The overcast sky and the stress of the last few days had taken their toll. She wanted only to sleep a bit longer, but it was probably already well past dawn. Sitting up, she rubbed at her weary eyes.

Beside her, Ruger had obviously just woken as well. He was still rolled up in his blanket, his relaxed face even more handsome when not pinched with tension. Last night, he'd insisted on sleeping next to her, and thankfully it was one argument Quin hadn't pushed.

After the explosion and up until bedtime, the two men had fought as she worked on the trap. Quin made the case for letting her go. Ruger barely said anything, his shoulders hunching with every argument from Quin, his expression rock-solid.

At one point, Ruger had looked like he might agree to her release, but then his stormy gaze had rolled over her in a mixture of longing and frustration. He'd held her gaze for a long moment before turning back to Quin and refusing to talk further. Was he keeping her here just because she could trap Jared or could there be more to his stubbornness? The questions about his motives never seemed to end.

As Alyna looked beyond Ruger's body, her heartbeat quickened. An empty bedroll lay on the ground where Quin should be. Taking a slow breath, she willed her heart to calm. Maybe he'd gone off to relieve himself or look for food. He'd said he wouldn't leave her here alone.

She slipped out of her sleeping bag and tugged on her shoes, then searched the campsite for tracks. The only ones she found headed back toward her original campsite. Would Quin have gone there to grab something? If he'd known Jared in school, perhaps he didn't fully understand their fears.

"I guess your boyfriend left." Ruger shook off the blankets.

She glared at him. "He's not my boyfriend."

"Does he know that?"

Ugh. Talk about focusing on the wrong thing. "We need to find him."

Ruger raised his eyebrows, clearly indicating Quin was on his own.

"Well, I'm going to find him."

"Don't—"

"Don't what?" She whirled on him, emboldened by the fact he hadn't yet grabbed the rifle. He trusted her, maybe more than he should. "Don't do it or you'll shoot me? I know. You've been threatening me for days, and it's not like I don't believe you. Sometimes you're as hard as stone. I know you'll do what needs to be done, but so will I." She turned her back on him. "I'm going to find my friend. You can try to stop me, but you *will* have to shoot me."

The cloud cover created extra shadows as she eased into the forest. A glance over her shoulder showed Ruger following behind, the rifle slung over his shoulder. She couldn't decide if his presence was comforting or not.

The gray day kept them hidden during the hike and as they circled to assess the safety of the campsite. No one was here, but something was different. A bright blue piece of paper, similar to the paper in one of her journals, was taped to the front support pole of her tent.

She crept up to it slowly. It was a note...addressed to her. Her lip trembled as she detached it and read the words.

Alyna, so nice to finally know your name. My gratitude to Quin for the information. I'm sure by now Ruger has told you who I am and where I've been recently. Somehow I don't think I have to convince you what I'm capable of, but if you don't bring me the jump drive, then I'll be forced to show you, using Quin. Meet me at sundown at what remains of your claim site.

Her gut lurched, threatening to heave out bile from her empty stomach. She sank to her hands and knees, flattening the note on the ground between her palms. Jared had taken Quin who had only come back to check on her.

As her swirling stomach settled, she looked around, suddenly feeling exposed despite Ruger watching her back. What if Jared was keeping close to the area?

Clutching the note in her fist, she jumped up and shoved it at Ruger. He took it, read, and narrowed his brows. "Why would Quin be so stupid?"

She snatched the note out of his hand. "This isn't Quin's fault. Jared is demented. This is all a joke to him."

"No. He's dead serious. He thinks being flippant about Quin will scare you."

"He's right about that."

"And he addressed the note to you as a way to scare me."

"Why would he have any reason to think you'd worry about me?" *She* didn't even know if Ruger cared about what happened to her.

"Because I wouldn't let someone who's innocent get hurt. He knows I'm not like him."

Was that it? She peered at his face. The emotions raging there betrayed him. He had some sort of feelings toward her, but they couldn't compare to his all-consuming search for the truth. She pushed her shoulders back. She wouldn't let Quin be a casualty in Ruger's war. "We've got to rescue him."

"Alyna, think about it. Jared picked sundown because after he kills us, he can dispose of our bodies without anyone, like a pesky claim jumper, seeing. Then he'll take the jump drive and be in the clear. No one will ever know what happened to us."

Much as she didn't want to admit it, he might be right. Plus, the desperate way he was staring into her eyes made her want to cradle his cheek in comfort. She pushed the impulse to the far reaches of her mind. Ruger might be willing to sacrifice Quin to find his mother, but she wasn't. She blew out a frustrated breath. "Okay. It's still early. Let's press Pause on this argument. If Jared wants the drive so badly, something must be on it. You know him better than anyone. Any chance you can break the password?"

"I could try."

"I've got my laptop, but I'll need a power source."

"Not a problem if you've got a car charger."

She nodded, for once leading the way into the woods. Finally, a course of action they could agree on. If they knew why Jared wanted the drive, maybe it would give her ammunition to get Quin back.

~

Ruger sat on his hands in the driver's seat watching Alyna log onto her computer. This whole situation had left him feeling like his hands were tied. Throughout his childhood, he'd learned that going against Jared never worked out well. Every time Ruger tried, Jared would escalate the stakes until Ruger gave in. Jared always won, and he always would because Jared was willing to die rather than give in. This time, Ruger had thought the playing field would be equal because he also was willing to die to find the truth. But could he make that decision for others? For Quin? For Alyna?

Turning his attention back to the one thing he could do, he watched Alyna's delicate hands resting on the keyboard. "I tried *Jared* just in case he was that stupid. What else should we try?"

Good question. If this jump drive concealed evidence of his mom's death, maybe it was her name. "Try *Elaine*."

She typed it in. A red text box popped up saying the password was incorrect.

"Maybe Mom's middle name. Try *Maude*."

Still incorrect.

"What about an old girlfriend?" Alyna asked.

"Could be." Jared hadn't dated many girls—his type was hard to find. He wanted a perfect body attached to a smart brain, yet he didn't want a girl to ever challenge him. "There was this one girl. She lived in a town about an hour away. I think her name was Phoebe."

Alyna typed in the name. The aggravating red box popped up again.

"Maybe we're thinking about this all wrong. Jared seems like a guy who is into himself. The password will be something important to him. What's his middle name?"

"Nicholas."

She tried it. "Nope."

Ruger pulled his hands out to run them through his hair. Although only a few years younger than Jared, he'd never felt like they'd known each other as brothers should. Jared had kept his distance. They didn't do anything together, except for the time when Ruger was ten and their mom forced them to take karate. She wanted to take it for self-defense, so she hauled them along. Come to think of it, the grizzled old instructor teased Jared about his ferocious fighting. He'd said, "You fight like you're wrestling down the only meal you'll get for a week, like a little jaguar." The instructor called him Little Jaguar for rest of the year. At the time, Ruger couldn't tell if Jared was proud of the nickname or insulted. Maybe a little bit of both.

"Try *Little Jaguar*."

Alyna gave him a curious look, but she typed it in. "No."

"Of course, he wouldn't want to think of himself as little anymore. Try just *Jaguar*."

She typed it in, then gasped. "It worked!"

A directory containing the names of two files appeared. Both were pictures. Alyna hovered her cursor over the first one. Her eyes sought his, their cobalt depths a swirling mixture of compassion and sadness. "Are you ready?"

Ruger imagined building a solid steel cage around his heart. Whatever he saw had already happened. Seeing a picture wouldn't affect reality. If only that made him feel better. He nodded that he was ready, knowing it was a lie.

She clicked and an image of rocks filled the screen. The backdrop was a sheer wall of sandstone. In the foreground, a river cut through a valley with sandy soil, not grassy, as though the river still overran its banks often. The area looked vaguely familiar.

He was still trying to place it when Alyna let out a small cry. "What?" he asked.

She pointed to the lower left corner of the picture. He'd missed it because the color matched the rocks so closely—the toe of a women's dress boot. Just the toe. The rest of the foot appeared hidden by the ground, which meant it was probably in the ground. He was looking at a grave.

He gripped his chest as the muscles clenched tight. A body was on the screen. Jared had buried a body. His mom really was dead.

Alyna spoke in a barely audible tone. "Did your mom have boots like that?"

"I don't know. Maybe. Every woman has boots in Colorado."

"I recognize this place from scouting claim locations." Alyna traced the short portion of river in the photo. "It's an eastern tributary of the Aruwa River. This cliff has some pristine fossils in it. I don't know whose property it is, though. Probably the same people who own Big Blue, an amazing aquamarine deposit. Quin never could get permission to mine it, but it sits right down the river."

Ruger's heart sank as the pieces all fell into place. He knew who owned all that property—his father. Jared had buried their mom in a place he knew Dad would never sell.

"Do you want to see the other picture?"

He didn't think he could handle it, but he had to know. Steeling himself against the tears, he gave one determined nod.

Alyna pulled it up. As his eyes scanned the image, he let out a captive breath. It was almost identical to the first, just from a slightly different angle. He swallowed past the lump in his throat. "We need to go find the..." Grave? Body? He just couldn't say it.

"But to get there we have to go around Mt. Pasaqua. It would take several hours to get there and then back. We won't make it by sundown."

Ruger shrugged. "Jared won't do anything to Quin until he gets what he wants. If we don't show, Jared will make contact again."

Alyna slammed her laptop closed. "I'm not willing to take that chance." She pulled the drive from the port. "We've seen the pictures. We don't need the drive anymore. Let's just give it to him."

Ruger tapped his foot. Right now, he wished he was alone to follow up this lead. But without Alyna, Jared would have taken the jump drive, and Ruger would have nothing. Even so, he snatched the drive out of her hand. "And once Jared has it, he won't need you or Quin anymore. You won't save Quin. You'll get him killed, along with yourself."

"So how do you think we're going to save him?"

Ruger bowed his head, ashamed at how little he cared about Quin's fate. His mom was all that mattered. He'd failed to rescue her from Jared back then. Now he had to go find her.

"That's what I thought. Your little plan includes sacrificing Quin. I can't do that."

His plan had only ever been to find his mom and make Jared confess. Neither Quin nor Alyna should have been a part of this. "Once we know for sure my mom is there, we can stick to the original plan. Trap Jared and push him to confess."

Alyna shook her head. She reached for the drive, but he swiped it away and got out of the car. As he came around to her side, she jumped out, glaring at him, looking much like a little jaguar herself.

But her size was no match for his, and she knew it. He side-stepped around her. Finding the site would be easier with her to guide him, but he'd been there as a child. It couldn't be that hard to locate. He strode off into the woods, throwing his last words over his shoulder. "If you're not going to come with me, then at least stay here where you're safe."

She yelled after him, "I should have known better than to trust a felon."

He kept moving. The words cut deep, but she was right. The

pre-prison Ruger would never have turned his back on them to reach his goal. Prison had changed him more than he wanted to admit. With each stomp of his feet, one tragic question thumped against his heart. How was it that he was doing worse things after meeting Jesus than he'd done before?

TEN

As Alyna stood alone by the car, Ruger stiffened his back and kept walking. She let a frustrated growl roll off her tongue. He was actually leaving Quin to endure whatever Jared had in mind. Good thing for Ruger she wasn't so cold-hearted or she would have shot him the first night he stole from her.

After the forest swallowed Ruger's cowardly form, she paced in a circle. What was she going to do? What *could* she do with no weapons against Jared? Then again, a rifle wouldn't help since Jared had a pistol and was definitely more likely to use it.

She needed a plan. With a glance up at heaven, she hugged her laptop and started walking back to the campsite. *Lord, I lost Dad four years ago almost to the day. Don't let this be the year I lose Quin. Help me.*

No idea sparked in her mind. Could the Lord mean for her to sit here and do nothing? When she reached the camp, she paced some more, kicking Ruger's blanket during one of her circles. As it settled back down to the ground and covered her laptop, an idea came to her. She would hesitate to say it was from the Lord because it was fairly deceptive. The jump drive Ruger took with him had a simple, plain black casing, and she had an identical one in her laptop sleeve. As a plan took shape, she glanced at her watch. She had just enough time to get to the meeting site first.

Three hours later, Alyna stood behind the trunk of a large pine tree, trying to convince herself she wasn't cowering. Her ears were attuned to every sound around her. The hoot of an early-rising owl, the rustle of a squirrel rushing up a nearby trunk, the sigh of the wind disturbing the leaves—all normal evening sounds. She kept her breathing even and slumped against the tree, settling in to wait.

Only half an hour later, a rhythmic crunching noise brought her standing straight to attention. The unmistakable sound of footsteps grinding dead leaves onto rocks. From the other side of the clearing, a dark head appeared.

"Quin!" She stepped around the tree.

His eyes met hers in a look of apology. She tried to give him a supportive smile, but was afraid it came out fake. This wasn't his fault.

Quin held up his hands, which were fastened tight in front of him by a black cord. Behind him, Jared broke through into the fading sunlight, his messy blond hair giving off the same reddish highlights as Ruger's. Maybe the brothers weren't as different as she'd once assumed.

Jared's brow wrinkled. "Where's Ruger?"

Alyna pursed her lips at the question. Lying with ease wasn't an option. Not only would it hurt God, but she wasn't any good at it. Jared would see right through her. "Ruger left."

Jared snorted. "Coward."

My thoughts exactly. Pushing her shoulders back, she took a step forward. Jared's total confidence in this situation infuriated her. "He could be getting the sheriff as we speak." If only that were true.

"Not likely, girlfriend." Jared drew out the last word, long and low, until it sounded like a curse word. "Ruger wouldn't trust a cop. For good reason." Jared stepped closer to her. "But he is full of surprises. Like why he would leave you to face me on your own. Without even a weapon."

Sucking in a quick breath, she sent up a prayer for strength. The only weapons she needed were her brain and the Lord.

Jared took a giant step closer, then another until he was only a foot away. She smelled sweat and sulfur on his skin. His dark eyes stared down at her, a slightly lighter shade than Ruger's, but somehow colder.

Her jaw twitched. *Focus on the plan.* She had to keep it together.

"So where is the jump drive? Or would you like me to strip-search you for it?"

She swallowed hard to steady her voice. "I've hidden it. I'll tell you where it is when you let Quin go."

His expression went from amused to lethal in a flash. "Who the hell do you think you are?" His gun hand shook. "You have no power here. You're just like every other stupid woman. So tiny." He slammed his shoulder into hers. She stumbled backward. "So weak, and yet you think I'm going to take orders from you. Maybe wimps like Ruger let you get by on sheer personality..." His gaze wandered the length of her body. "But not me. I'm fully willing and prepared to take what I need. Be glad all I need is the drive right now."

The hatred in his eyes went beyond her. Was he even seeing her? He clamped a hand around her chin, digging his fingers into her jaw.

Without looking back, he raised the gun and pointed it over his shoulder, directly at Quin. "Take me to the drive, now."

She couldn't nod, so she squeaked out the word "Okay."

When he let go, she rubbed her sore jaw.

Jared drew in a deep breath, plastering on his calm veneer

again, but all the tiny hairs on her body stood on end. The monster hovered just beneath the surface, a breath away from killing them both. She needed a miracle to trick him and get out alive. "This way."

She led him to a steep slope littered with fallen rocks. Not so steep the fall would mean death, but probably a broken bone or at the very least a long walk back to the top.

Leaning over the edge, she pointed straight down at a rock ledge sticking out from the surrounding rubble about four feet down. "I hid the jump drive behind a large boulder on the ledge."

She backed away, praying he would go after it himself and let them go. But Jared reached out to grab her arm. "Oh no. I'm not going down there." He pointed the gun at her face. "You are."

She crossed her arms over her chest. "Do you think I'm stupid? You're going to kill us sooner or later anyway."

"Brave girl with your own life. What about his?" Jared turned away from her and locked one hand behind Quin's neck, shoving the gun up under Quin's chin. "Better later, don't you think?"

Jared's calm, sarcastic demeanor scared her as much as his earlier rant. His face radiated determination. She and Quin were obstacles to be disposed of at any cost. She'd have to do this his way.

With slow measured steps, she slid down to the narrow ledge, leaning back to keep her balance. She reached behind the boulder, grabbed the empty jump drive, and held it up for Jared to see. As she'd hoped, his excitement overrode his caution. Rather than tell her to bring it up, he knelt to reach for it as he placed the gun flat on the ground, although his grip on it never wavered.

Stretching his arm out, he leaned forward. Just before he could grab the jump drive, she dropped it and latched on to his wrist. Leverage was her best friend now.

Surprise lit in his eyes as she yanked hard.

He teetered on the edge, trying to lean back.

She threw her body weight into pulling. One tug, two, then...the last yank dragged him over the edge. She leaned out of the way as his body soared above her.

She opened her hand, but on the way down, Jared reversed their tug-of-war, grabbing her wrist like a vise. He would make sure she went down with him. She braced her feet, but she wouldn't be able to fight against gravity with his extra weight.

A quick slide of crunching rocks, then strong arms encircled her waist. Quin?

But how could he? He was tied up.

The arms kept her from going over, but her wrist snapped taut. She cried out in agony. The hand that reached out to support her wrist had a jagged scar along the thumb.

Ruger!

Jared dangled from her wrist several feet above the rocky slope. Somehow, he'd kept his grip on the gun. As he hung, it swung wildly, firing once into the air.

Her wrist throbbed. Even Ruger's support wouldn't keep it from breaking soon. Using his thumb, Ruger dug under Jared's index finger, prying it loose.

A second later, Jared lost his grip and fell hard onto the rocks. The gun clattered next to him.

With one arm still around her waist, Ruger turned her around. He stroked her head as she clung to him. "I..." He cleared his throat. "At first, I thought you'd gone down too."

It must have looked to him like she'd fallen off a cliff to her death. Ruger placed a hand on her chin and titled her head up, his gaze seeking hers. The fear and relief in his probing eyes melted her heart. Just when she thought he might lean down to kiss her, he moved his hand to her damaged wrist, lifting it gently. He caressed the tender flesh, probing. She winced. "I don't think it's broken."

She bit her lip, trying to keep her hand from trembling. It had to be the adrenaline seeping out of her.

Movement below drew her attention. On the rocky slope, Jared twisted to a sitting position. His right hand scrambled over the rocks, searching for the gun. "We need to go."

They climbed up, untied Quin, and disappeared into the twilight of the forest. Ruger slowly led the way back to camp, his outline strong and steady for her to follow in the descending darkness.

As they walked, a weak filter of moonlight broke through the trees. Not much light to walk by, but just enough to create shadows everywhere. The woods she had loved for so long now held unknown dangers. Had Jared gone back to wherever he was camped, or was he trying to track them, watching and listening for their trail?

She swiped stray hairs out of her face, and rolled her shoulders to ease her tight muscles. She had to stop building Jared up into some evil supervillain. He was scary enough already.

Her thoughts turned from Jared to Ruger. His strong arms had wrapped around her, fighting to keep her upright. His chest had pressed into her, covering her back. She wondered what could have been between them under different circumstances. But she needed to get a grip. This was still the guy who'd kidnapped her. Coming back to save her was purely out of guilt, right?

"So, now that Jared has the jump drive, he'll leave us alone." Quin had been silent for most of the hike, and sounded hesitant, like he'd rather be alone. He walked with his back hunched, retracted in on himself.

"Yeah, about that." Alyna glanced back at Quin. "Jared doesn't have the jump drive."

He gave her a sudden frantic look. "It fell down the cliff with him."

"No, it didn't," Ruger said. Alyna glanced at him as he tugged the actual drive from his pocket and held it up.

She heard Quin stop walking. One look back at him, and she stopped too. His eyes had gone wide and wild. Fear etched lines in his forehead and tightened his mouth. "He won't give up. He'll never leave us alone until he has that. We have to give it to him."

"We can't." Alyna reached out to rub his arm.

He shook her off. "You don't get it. He won't stop. It's not worth it." Quin glared at Ruger. "Justice isn't worth our lives." He pressed his hands to his temples, turning to Alyna. "It's not worth your life."

She frowned. His concern was certainly appropriate. The fear had almost overwhelmed her as well. "If the person in those pictures is dead, it was worth their life. I can't ignore that."

"How do you know there are pictures on there?"

"We managed to break the password on the drive."

"You *looked* at it." In the soft moonlight, Quin turned deathly pale. "What did you see?"

Ruger bowed his head. The possibility of what the pictures meant had taken a toll on him. Dark circles and tight lines rimmed his eyes. Alyna cleared her throat. "A grave, I think. A rock formation in the background with a pair of boots that seem to be half buried in the ground."

Quin lunged for the drive still in Ruger's hand, but Ruger crooked his elbow and shoved him back. Quin glared at him. "Jared will be able to tell you looked at it. Give it to me. The only way we're going to survive now is if we destroy it."

Ruger stuck the drive in his pocket, then advanced on Quin. He shoved him with both hands. Quin staggered back, shocked. Ruger spoke through a clenched jaw. "That could be my mom's grave. Her disappearance means nothing to you, but it crushed me. I didn't leave the house for two weeks because I was afraid she might come back when I was gone. For years, I had nightmares of her calling out to me, begging for help, but I was trapped, unable to get to her. And then even my dreams of her grew fuzzy because I started to forget what she looked like, how she sounded, what she smelled like. I have nothing left of her except to find out where she is. Nothing will stop me from finding her!"

Quin responded in a mousy voice without making eye contact. "You don't even know if it's her." His gaze sought Alyna for support. "It might not be her."

She could barely speak through the thickness in her throat. Ruger had been through so much already. Maybe it would be better if he didn't have to carry the memories of finding his mother with him for the rest of his life. "What if we made copies, then turned the pictures in to the sheriff?"

"No!" both men answered in unison. *Weird.*

Alyna narrowed her eyes at Quin. Ruger didn't trust the sheriff because he'd been friends with Jared. Quin had known both Jared and Sheriff Hank. Did he have the same reason for not trusting the sheriff?

As if he could sense her question, Quin said, "Even if the sheriff comes for Jared, he could easily disappear into the mountains. Then we wouldn't be able to come up here without fearing Jared would show up. No more prospecting, Alyna. If we don't deal with Jared ourselves, we'll be looking over our shoulders forever."

Alyna tugged out her ponytail holder, scooped up her hair, and twisted it into a bun. "But we don't even have a claim right now to work."

"I could help with that." Ruger grabbed her uninjured wrist.

She looked down at his gentle fingers. For the first time, she didn't worry about whether she should brush him off. He'd come back to help her. No matter what prison had done to him, he was still a decent man deep down.

"We own lots of property around here. Help me find my mother and I'll make sure my dad finds you another claim."

Ruger released her, and the cool air felt more frigid on her skin. She tugged her jacket out of her backpack before glancing at Quin. "You agree?"

"On one condition." Quin faced Ruger. "If it's not your mother, then you give this up and let us go."

Ruger shook his head. "I can't promise that."

"Quin, you can't ask him to give up looking for his mother."

Quin's jaw worked in frustration. With a glare, he turned away. A niggling of guilt slithered through her stomach. It felt like she was being asked to choose between them. Was she minimizing Quin's attempt to get them out of this? Were they still kidnapped or would Ruger allow her to walk away like he did earlier? She was surprised at how little that last question mattered to her. Her emotions were jumbled and out of whack, and she wasn't acting like herself. But then again, neither was Quin. He wouldn't even meet her gaze.

ELEVEN

Ruger rolled over in the blanket, the bright sun yanking him from a simmering nightmare. Alyna lay next to him with her eyes still closed, her brow and cheeks smooth in sleep. If only she could look this peaceful all the time, but he'd given her much cause for stress lately. He'd imported the biggest bully of the prison yard straight into her mountain playground.

The rifle still sat near the top of his blanket. Although he continued to carry it and was ready to use it as a threat if necessary, he sensed the subtle shift in the air. After all he'd done to her, Alyna had defended his right to find his mother. They were going to do this together.

Glancing to the other side, he found Quin sleeping where Ruger had insisted he stay. Last night, Quin had wanted to switch places to sleep next to Alyna, but Ruger wouldn't give up the spot. He'd half expected Quin to be gone again this morning, and it would have been a relief. Despite the fact they had agreed about not contacting the sheriff, Ruger didn't trust Quin's motives. Was Quin just trying to protect Alyna? Even so, what kind of guy would suggest that Ruger just forget about what happened to his mother? Either Quin didn't have an ounce of compassion or his fear had completely taken over. No matter which was the case, it made Quin a potential problem.

Even though Ruger would have no qualms about leaving Quin to fend for himself, Ruger was stuck with him because Alyna wouldn't leave him behind. And if Ruger tried to go it alone, the same thing as yesterday would happen. Guilt would nag and eat at him until he turned back to make sure Alyna was safe.

He rolled over to look at her again. The soft skin of her cheek brushed the sweatshirt she used as a pillow. The loose waves of auburn hair flowed down her shoulders, the ends tucked into the sleeping bag. The curve of her exposed neck. She was beautiful, no doubt about it, and even quietly graceful in her own way, but there was more to her than just beauty. Her heart was fierce. They were both willing to sacrifice for the ones they loved, alive or dead.

Ruger heard Quin stir behind him. He didn't bother to look. Alyna had been ready to sacrifice herself for Quin. She obviously loved him, but in what way? Although she called him her best friend, Ruger didn't see a spark in her eyes when she looked at Quin. Not like the spark of defiance Ruger usually felt coming from her. No, she was comfortable with Quin. But was that love?

Alyna's eyes snapped open with a look of panic. She sat straight up, the sleeping bag wrapping around her like a cocoon. Her wild eyes found his. A quick glint of recognition sobered her, then she gave him a tiny smile. "Sorry, I had a bad dream."

Probably about being dragged over the cliff by Jared. With a resigned sigh, Ruger scrambled out of the blanket. "We should get going."

"Yeah." She swept her hair up into a messy bun. "Give me ten minutes."

While she got ready, Ruger trudged to the nearby stream to

fill their water bottles, relieved to not be holding a gun on them every minute and doing his best to forget what they might find at the end of their hike today.

After a granola-bar breakfast, they began walking with Alyna in the lead. She knew where the rock formation would be located. The area from the picture had looked familiar to him, but he couldn't place it. As they walked, though, he had the general impression they were heading in the direction of his father's property. His stomach clenched into a mass of throbbing knots. Would they find her? Had his mother been close all this time? He hefted his backpack farther up on his shoulders, the collapsible shovel weighing it down almost as much as this journey was weighing on his heart.

Several times along the way, Ruger glanced back to make sure Quin was still back there. He had been so quiet. No arguments, no complaining, not even one snide remark. Each time Ruger looked, Quin had his head down, eyes focused on the rocky, leaf-strewn slope.

After two hours of hiking, the ground beneath their feet changed from rocks to packed dirt. They had entered a river valley, one of the dry-run rivers that existed only to carry snow melt in the spring. A river valley was one of the few places in the mountains with enough soil to dig. His feet grew heavier with each step.

Alyna slowed her pace. "I think it's just ahead."

Ruger's stomach kept tightening until he felt like he'd swallowed a bowling ball. But nothing around them matched the picture yet. He continued to follow behind her. Alyna knew where she was going.

They walked up the dry river for several hundred yards that stretched into eternity. He trudged behind her, each planting of his foot taking him closer to the truth, each footfall heavier than the last. *Lord, give me strength.*

Finally, Alyna stopped and pointed to a rock outcrop protruding from the left side of the riverbank. "There. See the unique banding in the granite. This was an area I checked for future prospecting, garnets and sapphires actually. It's just a quarter mile upstream from the aquamarine deposit Quin tried to lease."

Quin had tried to make a claim on Dad's land? Dad had never mentioned anyone wanting to mine in the area. But then again, for the last two years he'd only talked to Dad during infrequent visits in prison. Mining rights wasn't one of their conversation starters.

Alyna moved to the side, then crouched on one knee. "Does this look like the angle of the picture to you?"

He knelt next to her and had to agree. This was it. His hands shook as he pulled the collapsible shovel out of his backpack. He snapped it open with a jolt.

Hovering with the tip ready to spear into the dirt, he hesitated. His body had the muscle power to do this, but inside he felt weak, his soul in danger of crumbling to dust. Was he really about to dig up his mother's grave?

He wouldn't make it through this unless he asked for more help. Something he hadn't done much since he'd left prison.

Clasping the shovel to his chest, he folded his hands on top of it and closed his eyes. "Dear Lord, You have brought us here for a reason. Only You know what lies in this ground. Help me to do what needs to be done and to accept the truth that You reveal. In Jesus's name. Amen."

A small answering amen came from Alyna. Quin said nothing, although when Ruger looked up, Quin's head was still bowed.

An infusion of power washed over Ruger, making him feel centered and strong. It wasn't peace—his stomach was still a mass of knots—but it was enough strength to give him the courage to continue. He stepped a few feet in front of Alyna and stabbed the shovel into the ground. The soft dirt surrendered to the force willingly, large clumps coming up with each thrust.

About three feet down, the shovel snagged on something. Using the pointed tip, he swiped dirt away to reveal the disintegrating remains of a red shirt. It was tattered and stained with dark brown splotches. He couldn't determine the style or even if it was a man or woman's shirt.

With the shovel suspended in the air, his muscles seized up. A shirt meant a person was underneath the shirt. He had to know if it was his mom, but was afraid to find out. He looked up, searching for Alyna's gaze.

He found only Quin. Quin shook his head and walked downstream.

Alyna touched Ruger's shoulder from behind. He turned to see calm resignation in her eyes, reminding him of the power he'd just felt. Odd how quickly it had faded. He sent up a silent prayer, then turned back to the hole he'd made. The fear of knowing wouldn't go away until he knew for sure.

He continued to dig, fast, but carefully. Within minutes, the shovel had unearthed a long, skinny bone—clearly human, probably from an arm.

Alyna gasped but said nothing.

Some distance behind him, Ruger heard the sound of Quin retching.

Ruger didn't look at either of them. Now that he'd started, he needed to finish this. His next shovelful exposed another long bone, followed by a rounded shoulder blade. He steeled his insides, building a dam to hold back the rushing river of sorrow, focusing only on the task. Slide the shovel horizontally, turn over the dirt, toss it to the side, and repeat. Over and over, he worked his way out, up and down until the whole of the horror was exposed.

As he dumped the last shovelful into the growing dirt pile, he took a deep breath and allowed himself to look at what he'd uncovered. The body wore a faded red shirt, ragged khaki shorts, or maybe it had been a skirt, and scraped-up leather boots. A few strands of muddy brown hair were twisted around the skull.

His mom had always worn her brown hair woven into a long braid. He remembered it smelling like her lavender shampoo. Could those small pieces be the only thing left of her braid? He walked along the length of the body. The features were larger, not quite as petite as he remembered his mom's stature. But he was thirteen when she'd disappeared. Had his mom just seemed smaller because he was smaller?

He looked Alyna up and down. She was probably about five foot three, within an inch of his mother's height. Imagining how tall Alyna would be if she lay down next to the body, he knew something was wrong. Not just from the height, but from what was missing. His voice was a low growl as he announced it to Alyna. "It's not her."

"What?"

"I said, it's not her. No aquamarine necklace, and this person is too tall."

Alyna gaped at him, then at the body. "Wait a minute. What's that?" She bent down and swiped dirt off an area near the tip of the right boot.

The glint of sunlight blinded him for a few seconds. When he could see again, Alyna was holding something round out for his inspection. The size of a candy Easter egg, it was polished and gleaming pale blue. "It's an aquamarine, but why would it be in there with her?"

He mulled it over for a minute. Then his body started to shake as he processed what it could mean. The gem was another sample from his mother's collection. He hadn't even noticed it was missing from the box.

There was only one reason it would be in with this unknown person—Jared had left it as a memento. And it meant the search for his mother wasn't over.

The slow walk back to camp was more somber than ever. Alyna trailed after Ruger, who had said nothing since she'd discovered the aquamarine. When he covered the body again, he stayed silent. When she said a prayer for whoever had been buried there, he remained quiet. Even when she'd told him she thought the specimen might be from the Big Blue Vein, he hadn't responded, merely turned to head back into the woods.

He was starting to scare her, but she couldn't blame him. His search was back at square one again. The acrid defeat hung so thick in the air, she could almost taste it.

Twilight dropped slowly over them like a blanket draped over the sun. She glanced back at Quin, who took halting steps with an uncharacteristic stiffness. His lips were pinched tight, brow squeezed, eyes focused on the dirty leaves underfoot. He mirrored her own feelings. Her heart was torn to shreds from the discovery of an unknown woman left to rot alone in the woods.

Close to Ruger's campsite, his footsteps slowed. She slowed her pace behind him. After another stuttering step or two, he stopped and hunched his shoulders. Had he heard something?

She waited, holding her breath, straining to hear. But only the sweet chirp of crickets and the low croak of frogs met her ears.

Just as she was about to tap him on the shoulder, he turned around. In an instant, his face changed from confused shock to predatory anger. He sidestepped her, charging at Quin.

Quin, still a few paces behind, stumbled backward. His feet slipped on the leaves, and he couldn't get the traction to evade.

Ruger fisted the front of Quin's shirt, pulling him up and close, chest to chest. "You!"

Quin let out an audible gulp.

"You knew!" His voice was more of a roar than a scream. "Before we left, you said it wasn't her."

Quin tried to pull away, but Ruger held tight. "No. I said it might not be her. That's not the same thing."

Ruger's bicep bulged from the effort to hold Quin, but the rest of his body stood rock-solid. Quin wouldn't get free unless Ruger released him. Alyna rushed over and grabbed Ruger's other bicep.

Ruger's jaw tensed, but he didn't let go. "He *knows* something."

"Don't you think if he knew something, he would have...?" Her protests died away as soon as she looked up at Quin. The guilt was written in pleading lines on his face. Had Ruger already interpreted Quin's expression, or had she only noticed because she knew him so well? Her already-tattered heart cracked in two. Should she try to protect Quin until she could discover what he'd done? She quickly glanced at Ruger. He appeared on the edge of giving in to a murderous impulse. Any effort she made to protect Quin wouldn't matter. Stubborn Ruger wouldn't give up until he heard what Quin had to confess.

Quin fixed his gaze on Alyna. "I wanted to tell you—alone."

She understood his fear. From day one, she'd known she couldn't control Ruger. Even so, he would listen to reason. Sometimes. She squeezed Ruger's bicep to get his attention. Keeping her voice low and smooth, she said, "Let him go, please. I promise, he isn't your enemy."

His eyes squinted shut, and she thought he would ignore her, but then slowly, finger by finger, he released his grip. Quin took a step back. Ruger stepped with him, staying close enough to grab him again.

Quin turned to focus only on Alyna. When he spoke, his voice had dropped to a whisper. "I know who she is."

A chill went down Alyna's spine. "The woman in the grave?"

"More of a girl really." Quin sucked in a breath, then coughed it out. He raked both hands through his hair. "Late one night in high school, I got a call from Jared. We knew each other from school. Well, everybody knew Jared, but we had never hung out together before. He said he needed my help. I imagined I'd be moving furniture or something, and I thought it would be my ticket to the in crowd." Quin barked out a laugh. "Turns out Jared had a massive problem."

A quick inhale from Ruger. Like her, he must have guessed where this was going. Her nerves twitched as she waited anxiously for Quin to continue.

"Jared's girlfriend lived in another town about thirty minutes away. She had sneaked out to see him that night. No one knew she was gone. Jared said they had a fight, and she ended up dead." Quin pulled on his hair so hard, Alyna thought he would yank it out. "That's how he said it, she *ended up* dead, like it was this big accident. But I saw the bruises on her neck, the blood on her head." A small retch, then Quin stymied the vomit, the back of his hand covering his mouth. "Jared needed me to take care of her body while he drove her car back to her house."

"Why would you help him cover that up?" Alyna asked.

A heap of shame settled into Quin's eyes. "Usually I try to forget why. Jared said if I didn't help, he'd tell the police I killed his girlfriend after a failed attempt to rape her."

That was it? One threat and Quin was covering up murder? A swarm of emotions assaulted Alyna—disappointment, sadness, anger—all vying for dominance. The Quin she knew wasn't capable of this.

Her turmoil must have shown on her face, because Quin

became frantic. "You don't know the things my mom said after the divorce."

She crossed her arms over her chest. What did his mom have to do with this?

"When Dad left her for the young hostess at the country club, she lashed out at all men, including me. I constantly heard how men were pigs, how they couldn't be trusted. She said God had made me deceitful because I was a guy. Back then, I was terrified she would believe a rape accusation." Quin paced back and forth, his eyes on the ground. "Plus, you know Jared. He can be extremely persuasive. I couldn't risk going to jail for the rest of my life." He stopped to gesture wildly with his arms. "And going to the cops wouldn't have brought the girl back."

His justification should have created some compassion for him as a scared teenager, but somehow it didn't stir anything. Her chest was already too full of emotion to add any more.

Ruger grabbed Quin by the shirt again. The way he flinched, she knew Ruger had fisted chest hair in with the cotton fabric. "You're sick. How could you dump some girl in the woods and go on with life like it never happened?"

"It wasn't easy. I created a part of me in my mind that had never done that, and I decided to only be him. The rest, I buried deep." His eyes darted around until they landed on Alyna, now with desperation deepening their hazel color. Probably the same desperation that had driven him to follow Jared's orders.

But to match Quin's distress, Ruger's body was taut with fury. Through clenched teeth, he growled, "Where is my mother?"

"I don't know." Quin shook his head so hard it lolled around. "I really don't. Jared told me to bury her as deep as I could on the family property along with the aquamarine, and to take the pictures. I couldn't bring myself to put any of her body in the picture."

The gemstone in Alyna's pocket weighed her down. If Jared

had insisted Quin place it inside his girlfriend's grave, it meant something to him. "You buried this girl after their mom was already gone?"

Quin nodded. "Ruger's mom left about the same time my parents got divorced. I remember my mom saying how she should have been the one to leave like Mrs. Westmoreland did, instead of letting my dad leave her."

Alyna pulled out the stone to gaze at its sky blue perfection. The Big Blue Vein meant something to Jared. And now she thought she knew why.

Ruger's fingers, still entwined in Quin's shirt, throbbed in time to his pounding pulse. The fingers of his other hand twitched with the desire to pummel Quin's face. The deep well of anger swelled up from his gut, swarmed through his veins, and flooded his blood with adrenaline. Quin had to know more, and Ruger would make him spill it.

He wrapped his other hand around Quin's throat, and his fingers compressed the soft flesh. With his thumb, he pressed into the tender trachea, cutting off Quin's oxygen.

Immediately, Quin went from a passive rag doll to a struggling victim. He pulled at Ruger's hand, but Ruger clutched tighter.

Alyna grabbed his arm, trying to yank it down, but he twisted out of her reach. She beat against his back. Her words were lost to him, but he knew she was pleading for him to stop. A tiny ache at the desperation in her voice distracted him. But his pulsing rage quickly pushed it away. Quin knew something more. He had to.

If he asked Quin one last time and didn't get an answer, he would...what? What would he do? A sick feeling slithered through his veins. Quin needed to use his breath to help Ruger find his mother or he didn't deserve to draw breath at all.

Ruger's words were thick with fury as he forced them out of his throat. "Where is my mother?"

Quin let out a raspy gasp. Ruger relaxed his grip so Quin could talk. "I..." He coughed and swallowed. "I don't know."

Liar. Quin had kept Jared's secret for too many years. He wouldn't have said anything now, except Ruger had cornered him. Quin obviously needed more motivation to talk.

Slowly, deliberately, Ruger squeezed his fist closed, watching the panic, the knowledge of impending death, draw inch by inch across Quin's face. Ruger closed his mind to the horror flashing in Quin's eyes. Instead, he shut his eyes to focus on the image of the young girl's skeletonized body. How Quin had left her alone. How her family had wondered about her all these years.

Quin deserved this...and more.

When Ruger opened his eyes, a different face floated before him. A man with a bald head, greasy brick-colored beard, and bulging eyes. The man he had almost killed in prison.

Before their confrontation, Ruger hadn't known the inmate nicknamed Redbeard, but they both ended up wanting the same set of weights at the same time. Almost as large as Ruger, Redbeard had decided to push a confrontation. Ruger tried to walk away, but Redbeard wrapped his arms around Ruger and shoved him into a weight rack.

Ruger shoved back, but Redbeard wouldn't let go. They struggled to punch and kick each other until Ruger grappled his arm around Redbeard's neck. Swiveling behind the inmate, Ruger locked his arm in place and refused to be bucked off. The guards had to pry Ruger's arm away just as Redbeard fell to the ground unconscious, his face and neck purple.

While choking him, Ruger hadn't seen Redbeard's face, but so much of this felt the same. The weak crush of the soft tissue, the fierceness of the hold, even the sense of it being justified. In prison, it was kill or be killed.

Except, he wasn't in prison any more.

The soft sob behind him suddenly came into loud focus. *Alyna.* "He doesn't know. Please stop."

A cold sweat broke out on his neck. She was right. Quin was close to the point of collapse. If he knew more, he would have confessed already. All Ruger was doing now was venting his anger.

He released his hold, afraid of how venting that anger felt.

Quin dropped to the ground, clutching his throat and wheezing. Alyna ran to Quin, put an arm around him, and continued to sob.

Guilt bubbled up, mixed with the adrenaline, and shot a burning slug of fire through his blood. Killing Quin wouldn't bring Mom back. Neither would killing Jared, but that one Ruger might actually enjoy.

As Alyna's sobs waned, Ruger sought escape. He didn't want to see the damage he'd done, the way she would look at him now, and he couldn't stand how close he'd come to losing complete control. He turned toward camp without a word, unable to comfort her, even unable to comfort himself.

TWELVE

Eventually, Alyna and Quin also returned to camp, where they found Ruger sitting hunched over on his blankets. She gave Quin an extra water bottle to soothe his throat, then sat alone on her sleeping bag. For the first time since Ruger had saved her from falling down the cliff, she thought about trying to swipe her car keys, or even his. She knew where both cars were parked. But something held her back.

Ruger deserved justice for his mother. She knew the emptiness of losing a parent. Her father's loss was a hole in her life that would never be filled. How much worse would it be not to know what had happened? His hollowness she could understand. It was the anger that scared her. The coldness in his eyes as he'd gripped Quin's throat.

And what about Quin? Could she blame him for giving in to Jared? Every time a sliver of compassion worked its way into her heart, she would picture Quin digging in the dark, then dragging the lifeless body out of the car, and shovel by shovel covering the dead girl in dirt, maybe even remembering the aquamarine at the last minute. But Quin wasn't that cold-hearted. She knew him. Didn't she?

Neither of these men were what they'd seemed to be. How was she supposed to know whom to trust?

Tugging out her ponytail, she ran a hand through her loose hair while digging out a granola bar with the other. The granola bar tasted like cardboard, but her body rejoiced at the calories.

As she crossed her legs, her pants bulged out from the aquamarine in her pocket. Why had Jared told Quin to leave it there? She could only come up with one logical reason. It was an inside joke for Jared himself. A reminder of his first kill buried with his second.

What if it *did* lead to Ruger's mother? Of all the stress of the last few days, one worry rose to the top of her mind. If Jared had killed his mom, and now realized they were getting close to finding her, all he would have to do would be to wait for them to show up at the grave.

They would have to be more careful while they searched, and she knew something that might help. A way to give them advanced warning if Jared tried to sneak up on them. She crumpled up the granola bar wrapper, stuffed it into her backpack, and got to her feet. "I need something from my car. I'll be back in a couple of hours."

Ruger turned tortured eyes to hers. "But it's almost dark."

"I'll be fine in the moonlight." She stayed firm, waiting for him to acquiesce. If he was expecting her to help after all he'd done, he'd have to give her some trust.

"What if Jared found your car?"

"I'll just have to take that chance." She had a feeling he was closer to where their mom was buried anyway.

"I'll go with you."

Ruger started to get up, but she put her hand up as a barrier between them. "No." A long pause before Ruger looked like he would speak again. She cut him off. "I just need a break from all the drama around here. I'll be fine."

Ruger's gaze dropped to the ground. No doubt he felt guilty for almost choking out Quin, which he should. And Quin didn't look like he had any fight left in him. She turned on her heels and left. But a niggling sense of hypocrisy followed her out of the camp. What would she have done if her father had disappeared? She already had anger issues brought on by those who said her father had wasted his life. Like his supposed colleagues, who were quoted in the newspapers saying that his obsession with the veil had been a fool's errand and it had crushed his career long before the church crushed his body. As if it were their right to judge. If she could have gotten her hands on them, she, too, might have been tempted to squeeze and squeeze until they couldn't utter another word. Even so, Ruger's anger was much more dangerous than hers.

The walk to her car was quiet, uneventful, and lonely. She felt more alone out here than ever before, and not the usual peaceful, serene kind of alone.

Digging through the trunk, she found her old miniature digital camera underneath some sample boxes near the back. It was her backup in case she filled her phone's memory with pictures and needed to take more sample photos. The date and time stamp on the photo counted as her proof of discovery for valuable specimens. This camera had been a faithful backup that now needed to be sacrificed.

By the glow of a small penlight, she grabbed a screwdriver and unscrewed the outer casing of the camera. Setting it aside, she peered down at the interior in the fading light. More screws held the back screen over the glass lenses. She couldn't get to them from this side unless she had a smaller screwdriver. Like the one in her eyeglass repair kit at her original campsite.

Her own advice to Quin to stay away from camp echoed in

her ears, but she dismissed it. Jared probably wouldn't be there, and it was worth the risk. She just needed to grab her tiny eyeglass kit. Two minutes maximum.

At the campsite, she crept over to the destroyed remains of her tent. She flipped back the right side and dug through the debris using the penlight. As she'd predicted, finding the kit took only a few minutes. She'd never worn glasses, but the screws came in handy for replacing ones lost from electronic devices.

She switched off the light, then headed a safe distance away before turning it on again. Sitting cross-legged and holding the flashlight between her teeth, she unscrewed the back screen and pulled out the battery. Beneath rested a reddish piece of glass, the infrared filter. She removed it and tossed it to the side, then quickly fit the camera back together. This was an easy hack that would allow the camera to see in infrared, giving her a rudimentary form of night vision complete with thermal imagery.

After flicking off the flashlight, she turned the camera on for a test. With her unaided eyes she could only see through the darkness for about two rows of trees. But on the screen, layer upon layer of trees stretched into the distance. *It worked!*

Twisting to the side, she panned over the campsite, now about fifty yards away. The detail she could pick out in the dark was amazing. A spare blanket crumpled in a pile. The flap of one corner of her destroyed tent as it blew in the breeze. Everything was a hazy blue, but astoundingly clear.

She jumped to her feet, swinging around farther to her left. At the apex of her arc, she stifled a gasp.

Outlined in glowing white on the screen was a human-shaped form, standing on the other side of the clearing.

The person stepped into the open.

She took a slow step back.

His head whipped in her direction. He'd heard her.

"Alyna?"

It was Jared. But how did he know it was her?

"Playing hard to get?"

She held her breath and refused to move, except to cover the small amount of light coming from the camera display. It was clear from the way his head swiveled that he didn't know exactly where she was.

"It has to be you. Ruger would be trying to kill me right about now."

She kept her mouth firmly shut. Let him think he'd heard a deer.

"I won't hurt you. I just want to talk."

No way would she fall for that line.

"You know, your boyfriend isn't as innocent as you think."

Was he talking about Quin?

"I don't know what he's told you about me, but Ruger has secrets."

She should have known this would be about Ruger.

"Did he tell you he hated our mom even more than I did?"

That was ridiculous. He was baiting her. She planted her feet, refusing to budge.

"She was leaving Dad. Tearing apart our perfect family. Well, at least *Ruger* thought it was perfect." He took a step in her direction.

Coincidence? Or had he locked on to her location? She sent up a quick prayer for protection. She noticed with some satisfaction that he limped a little. Must have been a hard fall down the cliff.

"Until he learned his beloved mother had a new life picked out already. A boyfriend she was going to marry who had a little boy, even. Ruger lost it. Who could blame him really?"

A breath caught in her throat. He was a liar. It wasn't true. It couldn't be.

"I'm pretty sure he blocked out the killing part. I found him with his hands locked around her throat. What else could I do? He's my brother. I had to protect him, so I buried her and never told him where. Ruger is looking for her, but he shouldn't. It will only implicate him."

Alyna opened her mouth to ask him about the Big Blue Vein and if their mom was there, but she slammed it shut just in time.

"Phoebe I'll take responsibility for, but Ruger killed Mom. Guess homicide runs in the family."

Did he know they had already found Phoebe? Jared took a step to the left. She released her trapped breath. *Let him search blindly, Lord.*

"I should never have covered up for him. In fact, I'm ready to come clean. We should both be in jail. But I'll need your help to make that happen. Take me to Ruger."

Uncertainty rippled through her stomach. Her heart pounded as her mind scrambled to make sense of things. Could any part of it be true? Was Ruger's search for his mother borne out of guilt? His sorrow over her disappearance appeared genuine, but could it be an act? Or had he blocked out the crime? The idea seemed ridiculous, but with Ruger's earlier behavior, she had to at least confront the possibility. And she had to admit she might not be completely objective. His search for justice for his mother had sparked a connection between them. She'd thought he searched to honor his mother's memory, but could his real motive be to destroy the evidence that pointed to him? After all, he refused to let the sheriff get involved, and he'd admitted he hadn't come looking for his mother until Jared had been released.

Jared took another step to the left, essentially putting his back to Alyna. This was her chance. Pointing the camera at her feet, she used it to avoid leaves and sticks so she could move silently away from him.

The last thing she heard before she left Jared behind was him saying, "If you trust Ruger, he'll kill you."

When she reached Ruger's camp, she hesitated before entering. Ruger paced along the length of the small clearing, and Quin sat on his sleeping bag, chin tucked on top of his knees. What a mess this situation was. She wrestled with the sudden desire to turn around, take her car, drive home, and hide under her bed. But even if she wanted to, she didn't have the car keys.

Ruger's agitation vibrated through the air with every pass he made along the length of the clearing. Another disturbing possibility occurred to her. Ruger might have insisted on keeping the sheriff out of it so he could draw Jared out, effectively killing the only other person who knew of his crime. It sounded at least possible, but it didn't *feel* true. Trouble was, right now she didn't trust her feelings.

Alyna stepped into the campsite. Ruger caught her eye, tension flowing off him in waves as relief lit up his face. In two quick strides, he came to her and pulled her into a hug. It took every ounce of restraint to keep from melting into his arms. But she needed to confront him. Up to this point, she'd been going on gut instinct regarding him. In reality, they barely knew each other.

"What took you so long? I—" Ruger cleared his throat, glancing at Quin. "We've been worried."

"I had to go back to my camp for a screwdriver."

Ruger sucked in a frustrated breath. "What were you trying to prove?"

His words struck a chord inside her. Deep down, she knew she'd wanted to prove she couldn't be intimidated by fear. She might have found another way, but the simplest path was to her old campsite, and she was stubborn.

"Jared could have hurt you."

He had no idea how close she'd come to Jared. She studied Ruger for a moment. His eyes held a mixture of fear and relief, and his mouth was set in a firm line. Was he worried about what Jared would do to her or worried about what Jared would say?

His hands settled at her waist, drawing her close. His gaze shifted to her lips, and his mouth parted. A swell of desire swirled in her chest. How did he do that to her so easily? Better question: why did he seem to only want to kiss her when he was frantic with worry?

Painfully aware of her own body's betrayal, and Quin watching them, she backed away. "Actually, I saw Jared."

Ruger grabbed her arms. "What?"

"But he didn't see me." She held up the camera. "I converted this to night vision."

Ruger raised his eyebrows and let go of her. "How did you do that?"

She shrugged. "It's not that hard."

He reached for the camera, dropped it onto her sleeping bag, then turned back to her. He gently swept a loose strand of hair behind her ear. "You're okay?"

She shook her head, dislodging the hair again. "He said some things."

"Like what?"

Ignoring Ruger, she turned toward Quin. "Did Jared ever hint to you that he'd killed before?"

"No." Quin leaned back on his hands. "He didn't even say he killed Phoebe. Just that it was an accident."

Ruger turned her around by the shoulders. "What's going on? Why are you asking Quin about this?"

Meeting his gaze, she took a deep breath and blew it out before answering. "Jared admitted to killing Phoebe, but he said you killed your mom. Jared claims he only covered up your mom's murder to protect you."

A low growl rumbled from Ruger's throat. "You don't believe that crap, do you?"

She merely raised her eyebrows. No way would she let him avoid answering by pushing the question back on her.

"I was in junior high, only thirteen. Jared was a senior."

He had a point. She'd forgotten Jared was five years older, which made him more likely to be the killer.

Ruger wiped a hand down the stubble framing his chin. "The night my mother disappeared, we had a fight. She said she wanted to leave my dad, which meant leaving us, at least for a while. I didn't want my family split up, so I yelled at her, told her she was being selfish. She just kept saying she didn't love my father anymore."

That was essentially what Jared had said. "Did you know she had a new boyfriend?"

His chest seemed to deflate. "She said they were going to get married, and I'd have a little brother. I didn't want another brother. I wanted things to go back to the way they were. After yelling at her, I went to bed. When I woke up, she was gone." His voice dropped to a husky whisper. "I never saw her again."

As he said those final words, he averted his eyes, evidently caught up in deep pain. Alyna shifted to catch his gaze. The raw, ragged agony in his eyes couldn't be faked. Ruger had never wanted his mother dead. Everything Jared had said was a lie. Fury burned through her blood. They needed to send him back to prison forever.

She grabbed Ruger's wrist and began tracing a soothing circle along the inside. "I think I know where she is."

Ruger looked from her hand on him to her eyes. "Where?"

"The aquamarine we found with Phoebe is from that Big Blue Vein that I've always wanted to mine, but couldn't. I think Jared put it in with Phoebe to remind him, as a mental link between her and your mother. Which means your mother is probably buried near there."

Quin jumped up from his spot. "That's on land owned by your father."

"I can take you there tomorrow," Alyna said.

"I thought Jared left the aquamarine just to taunt me in case I ever found Phoebe's body. But maybe you're right. Maybe it's a clue." As understanding sunk in, a gray cloud seemed to descend over Ruger's hopeful expression. Tomorrow they would search again for his mother. If they found her, it would all be over, but the closure would likely bring its own harsh reality.

Alyna squashed the desire to comfort him. Instead, she let go of his hand and slid into her sleeping bag. Although she believed Ruger, her doubts had left her reeling. He hadn't told her before about the fight with his mother, or his mother's boyfriend.

After a few minutes of tossing and turning, she looked over to catch him staring at her. A spark lit inside her chest, but she quickly doused it with a healthy dose of fear. She didn't know enough about the man behind those smoldering brown eyes.

Jared didn't try to approach the side of the cliff stealthily. He was hidden by the darkness, and the noise Adam Schroeder made while chipping away with his rock pick would cover all other sound. At least he assumed it was Adam. Jared had meant to come check the Big Blue Vein sooner, but had been distracted by the hunt for Ruger and Ruger's new girl. When Alyna slipped away from him earlier—he was sure she was there—he realized that they might be closer to finding Mom's body than he'd anticipated.

He'd been too late to stop them from discovering Phoebe, but that didn't mean they would make the connection to the aquamarine vein. Ruger hadn't been out here since their childhood. Alyna and Quin, on the other hand, might have enough experience in the area to figure it out. If they did, he needed to have a surprise waiting for them.

The backside of the mountain sloped gently down toward the river, depositing him into the open floodplain next to the water. With a quick glance at Mom's spot, he continued on, balancing carefully on the log bridge. The river below ran fast and deep for this time of year, probably due to the thundercloud on the crest of the mountain last night.

Click! Clang! Wearing thick work gloves, Adam kept up a steady rhythm as he struck the stone.

Once on the other side of the river, Jared slid one hand along the cliff face and walked the short distance on the worn narrow path between the river and the cliff.

Finally, Adam noticed Jared standing just inside the circle of a spotlight pointed at the cliff face. The rock pick fell to Adam's side and the sudden silence was a relief.

A few feet away, Jared planted his feet and drew his body to its full height. "Surprised to see me?"

Adam's face showed more than mere surprise. His eyes were wide with fear, the pulse in his throat throbbing.

Jared smiled. Adam might actually be smarter than he looked. "You have nothing to say to the man who allowed you to come mine here?"

Adam rubbed the back of his neck with one gloved hand. "Uh, you're supposed to be in jail."

"It's amazing what the legal system can do for those who are persistent." Jared folded his arms, purposely making his chest look larger. Adam's eyes went even wider. "I'm glad you brought up the whole jail thing. It's sort of awkward to start this kind of conversation, but I remember having an arrangement with you while I was in jail."

Adam sucked in his cheeks.

"We agreed you could mine this area if you put half the

profits in my bank account. You've obviously been mining, so where's my money?"

Adam's fist tightened around the handle of the rock pick.

Jared ignored the implied threat. "And now here's the real awkward part. You don't have it because you thought I wouldn't be coming back to collect my money, at least not anytime soon. Can't blame you exactly. In fact, it's something I would have done."

Adam's shoulders relaxed, but he kept an iron-like grip on the pick. If he decided to use it, he'd find out all the tricks Jared had learned in prison about fighting.

"The good news is, I have a way for you to pay me back. It involves some dirty work, but afterward you can mine this claim forever, keeping our original fifty-fifty split, of course."

For a brief instant, Adam's eyes returned to normal, then he squinted at Jared. "What do I have to do?"

"My brother, Ruger—he looks a bit like me except shorter and less attractive—is trying to take over this claim. If you let him, he'll take it from both of us. I'm going to be out there searching for him, so I need you here to defend it." He paused for a moment to give his next words more weight. "Defend it with deadly force. I promise Ruger will kill you if he gets the chance. So don't let my brother or anyone who comes with him leave here alive. Can you do that?"

A brief hesitation. Adam looked up at the tips of several rough aquamarines sticking out of the cliff. When he looked back, he gave a crisp nod.

I knew I liked this guy.

Adam lifted one shoulder. "I'll have to be out here all day?"

"Yes."

"Okay, I'll go into town and find someone to run the hardware store for a while."

"Whatever you need to do, do it. If Ruger sets up camp on

this claim, you'll never get near it again." Jared lowered his arms and took a step backward, confident Adam's greed would take care of the rest. "Oh, yeah." Jared winked at Adam. "Don't forget to secure the site before you go."

Adam scoffed. "Always do."

Most prospectors had some form of protection for their site when they were gone. Hopefully it would be enough to hold Ruger if he showed up before Adam got back.

THIRTEEN

The morning sun drifting through the trees did nothing to brighten Ruger's mood or lighten his steps as they hiked. Alyna had said the Big Blue Vein would be several hours away, and every step felt like he was dragging a ball and chain around behind him. Since coming out of prison, the iron shackles had never left him; they'd just moved from his wrists to his heart.

The suspicious glint in Alyna's eye each time she looked his way was proof enough that prison had changed him permanently. He couldn't be trusted. Last night, he'd barely slept, haunted by the image of Quin's bulging face, the terror in his eyes, his open mouth desperate for air he couldn't inhale. After that, Ruger couldn't blame Alyna for thinking he might have killed his mother. Or for wanting to go back to her car alone.

Trudging uphill behind her, he admired the way she led them with confident strides. This was her element, the place where she belonged. He didn't understand why she intended to continue her father's archeological work when she so clearly loved this. He could relate. The rugged mountains, the rocky peaks, the crystal blue sky—it was home for him too.

Glancing around at the trees, he wondered if they had wandered onto his father's property yet. Their mountainous real estate was vast and rugged. It would take him days or weeks if he had to search for the vein on his own. Thankfully, Alyna was still willing to help him.

The slope leveled out for a short distance, then plunged downward. The steep angle kept him leaning back to hold his balance and keep from falling backward into Quin. As they descended, his footing became less sure because the amount of rocks increased. Several outcrops of crumbling rock sat in isolated pockets. Obviously, none of them contained the Big Blue Vein since Alyna barely glanced at them. Although he'd gone gem hunting with his mother when he was younger, he still couldn't fathom what Alyna looked for when she searched for gems. For him, it would be hard to tell a plain rock from a rough gemstone.

Alyna broke through the trees onto a sandy shore and halted. Ruger stopped behind her while Quin edged around them. Quin had barely said a word since yesterday, and Ruger preferred it that way.

Alyna pointed at a rising cliff on the other side of a wide river. A huge log lay across the water as a bridge. "The Big Blue Vein is just on the other side of the river."

Ruger's stomach tightened into a twisted rope of fear. He'd been letting his mind wander, focusing on anything besides what they were actually here to do. Now he could no longer keep reality at bay.

A floodplain would be the only place to dig deep enough to bury a body. He slowly turned his eyes to the long expanse of sandy soil. The cliff side of the river would be too tight. His mother had to be here somewhere...beneath his feet.

Stuffing down his dread, he stripped the pack off his back and pulled out the collapsible shovel. As if his muscles remembered what they'd found yesterday, his arms trembled as he flipped the shovel open.

"Someone can help dig with this," Alyna said, holding up the flat end of her rock pick. "And somebody should scan the forest with the heat-sensing camera to make sure no one sneaks up on us."

She looked at Ruger with questioning eyes. He appreciated that she let him decide. It wouldn't sit well with him to let Quin dig test holes looking for his mother. "Give the camera to him."

Alyna handed it over. "It won't be as sensitive to changes in heat as it would be at night, but if you keep a close eye, you should be able to tell if something big is coming our way." Alyna turned back to Ruger and spoke in a soft voice. "What do you want me to do?"

A black hole engulfed his chest. What he wanted was for her to wrap her arms around him, to tell him there was no possible way his mother had been killed by his brother and abandoned in the middle of nowhere. If only she could tell him this wasn't really happening. He sucked in a sharp breath to push down the bile rising in his throat. "Let's start on opposite ends of the sandbar and just dig, I guess."

For several hours, he dug test holes, each time hoping not to find something, and each time hoping to find something. The bedrock was about five feet down, so they dug each hole to about four feet, which took a long time. And it took even longer for Alyna. Her pick could only make a hole down about two feet before she had to dig the rest by hand.

After several hours of quiet digging, the sound of a thump made him stop and turn to look. Alyna had fallen to her rear end, the rock pick landing beside her. She turned shocked eyes to meet his. "I, um, found something."

Ruger ran over. In the hole, a few strands of brown hair were attached to a hair band. Two outer strands twisted over a center strand—the remains of a long dark braid. Just like the braid his mother always wore. Had they really found her this time?

He took small scoops of dirt, easing his way down over the area where the woman's head should be. When the outline of white bone surrounding her eye sockets came into view, he had to step away. The memory of his mother's steady dark eyes pleading with him to understand on the last night they argued suddenly came back fresh in his mind.

The vein of aquamarine had pointed them here. But still, maybe it wasn't her.

Stepping back, he uncovered a little more to expose the raw bone of the spinal column and shoulders. Twisted around the base of the neck was a small gold chain with a dainty aquamarine charm. *His mother's necklace.*

The sight of it carved a deep pit into his heart. He stumbled over to the tree line and heaved out the granola bar he'd had for breakfast. His search was over.

He waited for relief to come, or at least a sense of accomplishment. Instead, his chest quaked as if the pit in his heart were a giant expanding sinkhole. He gasped for air at the pain in his rib cage, as if his bones had splintered into a million cracks and fissures that were splitting apart with every tiny movement.

Now he understood fully why he hadn't gone looking for his mother when he first suspected what Jared had done. Knowing the truth brought its own sort of closure, but reality hurt far worse than not knowing. In reality, there was no longer hope. No hope of his mother ever being alive again. No hope that Jared wasn't a heartless, selfish monster. No hope of this pain ever going away.

How would Dad take the news? After she'd disappeared, Dad never referred to her as Mom anymore, only Elaine. Ruger had taken it to mean Dad believed she had deserted both them and the new boyfriend. He would probably be shocked to know Jared had gotten to her first.

A soft touch made him flinch. Just one hand on his shoulder blade. Alyna was trying to comfort him, and he was torn between pulling away to grieve alone and throwing himself into her arms. So, he froze in place. If he didn't move, maybe he could calm the earthquake of pain threatening to rip his chest in half.

"Ouch!" The loud grunt came from behind. Alyna slipped her hand off his back. Wiping his mouth, he turned to look. Across the river, almost around the bend—at the same place Alyna had noted the aquamarine vein—Quin sat on the ground, his face contorted in pain.

An angry flush pulsed through Ruger's veins. While he was grieving, Quin was scoping out the aquamarine deposit, and now he must be trapped.

As Alyna hurried toward the log bridge, Ruger turned away again. Let her run off every time Quin yelped. What did it matter?

He looked down to see a water bottle she'd brought for him. After rinsing out his mouth and spitting to the side, he took a long drink.

With his head titled back, he caught sight of the hole he'd dug. The white sheen of bone contrasted with the leftover tendrils of her hair, held together only by a bright purple hair tie. Like a current flowing downstream, the adrenaline causing his chest to shake rushed to his extremities. His hands trembled violently. He pressed them into his eyes to keep the tears at bay, but they kept shaking.

He needed to do something...anything. Should he uncover the rest of her or leave her here until he had somewhere to take her? If he left her, Jared would certainly see the ground had been disturbed. Then he might take her somewhere else, somewhere hidden.

Ruger couldn't let that happen. He picked up the shovel laying by his mother's body and quickly uncovered the rest of the skeleton. This meager pile of bones was all that remained of his mother. They would have to take her with them, after Alyna took some pictures. He didn't think he could do it without breaking apart completely.

"Ruger!"

Alyna waved her arms at him from the other side of the river while squatting next to Quin. "I need your help."

Ruger gave a careless shrug. "Let him starve to death."

She stood to her full height and put both hands on her hips. He would have been amused in different circumstances and likely egged her on. Now he was too spent to argue. He placed a dark blue blanket over his mother's grave and stepped onto the log bridge. He'd probably need Quin's help to get her out of here anyway.

On the other side, Ruger squatted next to Alyna to assess the situation. Quin's leg was trapped by a large set of metal coon cuffs secured by a chain to a small tree. Another cuff lay on the rock nearby.

"Only one got his leg, but I can't get it off," Alyna said.

As much as he might enjoy ripping Quin's leg off, the tree appeared to be the weakest link. Trapped beneath the edge of the sheer cliff, it didn't receive enough sunlight to grow thick, merely tall.

Alyna had apparently realized that as well because she'd taken a sharp rock and tried to cut through it. Ruger had a better way. He stood and gripped the tree trunk about halfway up, then shoved it away from the cliff. It didn't need to break as far down as Alyna had been working; it just needed to break somewhere along the trunk, then they could slide the chain up.

When the tree had bowed enough, he walked his hands along it, pulling it down, increasing the stress. He couldn't go all the way because of the tangle of branches near the top. At the highest point he could reach, he squatted low, dragging the tree to the ground. The wood creaked and groaned.

He released it to stand halfway up, then he squatted again.

A loud creak, followed by a satisfying crack. The wood splintered about two feet above the ground.

After stretching his back muscles for a moment, he flipped the tree to the other side, working it back and forth to break it off. The green center was the strongest and hardest part to break through, but eventually it gave way.

He dropped the fallen tree to the ground with a grunt. In the sudden silence that followed, a heavy footfall sounded behind him.

Alarm skittered down his spine. Quin was supposed to be watching the forest, and between the rush of water in the river and the tree splintering, they wouldn't have heard someone approach.

Ruger slowly turned, expecting to see Jared. Instead, a man held a rifle to his eye, partially obscuring his face. *Wait a minute.* It was Adam from the hardware store. His narrowed eyes were meant to seem threatening, but the man was only about six feet tall. Ruger could take him—that is, if he could get the gun pointed away.

A sideways smile broke out on Adam's face. "Your brother said you might come. I just didn't expect you this early."

Alyna pushed around Ruger. "Mr. Schroeder?"

Adam's confident smile disappeared. "Alyna, what are you doing here? With him?"

"We've been looking for—"

"We're looking for gemstones." Ruger grabbed her arm as a warning, harder than he'd meant to if her surprised reaction was any indication. "Sorry, we didn't realize this was your claim." He worked hard to give a lighthearted chuckle. "And we're even sorrier our friend fell into your trap."

Adam narrowed his eyes. The guy didn't seem like a genius, but he also didn't seem to be buying Ruger's innocent act.

"But he should know—" Alyna started again.

Ruger pulled her into his chest, burying her face in his shirt to keep her quiet. He couldn't let her tell Adam about his mother's body. Jared probably hadn't told Adam all of his secrets. If Adam knew, it would only make it harder for Adam to let Alyna go. And the fatherly way he'd treated Alyna in the store gave Ruger hope that Adam wouldn't want to hurt her. "What you should know is that Alyna was just tagging along." Technically it was a misdirection, not an actual lie.

Adam twisted his mouth up and down, directing a gentle gaze at Alyna. *Good.* He was conflicted about what to do with her. Ruger could work with that.

"Why don't you just let her go, then you and I can talk about how we can make this up to you. I'm sure we can compensate you somehow."

At the word *compensate*, Adam's eyes flickered closed. He looked offended. Maybe Ruger had taken it too far. But then Adam gestured toward Alyna. "You shouldn't have been here anyway, girl. Go on, get out of here." Using the rifle, he gestured for her to go. "But don't come back. And don't tell anyone you saw me out here." The warning was low and punctuated with Adam smacking the rifle.

Ruger grabbed Alyna's shoulders and pushed her toward the log bridge. She hesitated, glancing back at him, then at Quin. Her eyes said that leaving tore her up, except he wasn't sure which one of them she hated leaving more. Him? Or Quin, who always seemed to need her? This time, it didn't matter. She just had to leave. "Go, please."

Adam grabbed her arm. Ruger tensed, ready to jump at him. But Adam merely guided Alyna past himself and closer to the bridge. With a defeated glance back, Alyna crossed the log and disappeared into the woods on the other side. Ruger released a tense breath. At least she'd gotten away. He'd trapped her in his own personal nightmare for too long. He wouldn't let it cost her any more than it had already. He glanced over at Quin. Scratch that, if anything happened to Quin, Alyna would consider it too high a price to pay.

FOURTEEN

Alyna took a dozen steps into the cover of the woods before her feet refused to go any farther. What was she doing? Ruger had fixed a terrified glance on her, given her a desperate plea to leave, and the strength to fight melted right out of her. She would have done anything at that point to ease the fear on his face—even walk away. But she couldn't just abandon him. Or Quin.

Would Adam really hurt them? Obviously, Adam had been mining the aqua, and from the look of the cliff side, he'd been at it for a while. If he was protecting the claim, then violence was a definite possibility. Or maybe he just wanted to scare them away?

A streaking hiss sounded behind her, followed by the crackle and pop of an explosion in the air. A flare.

Her heart sank. Adam was signaling someone, and it had to be Jared. She needed to get back there, but she couldn't do it over the log bridge. It was too exposed. She had to come at them from upstream. With a fresh shot of adrenaline energizing her, she carefully picked her way through the tree cover while keeping an eye on the river, searching for an easy place to jump across.

Several hundred yards later, the river depth dropped as the slower water fought for every inch it cut into the tough granite bedrock. Around a curve, she discovered the reason for the slow-down—a natural dam of rocks. She waded through the knee-deep water behind the dam, then dashed into the safety of the trees on the other side.

She crept through the foliage for a hundred yards before coming up against the area where the water had cut deep and the beginnings of the cliff were evident. If she followed on the north side, she'd end up at the top of the cliff. She stayed south, following the river and edging along the cliff as it grew to her waist, over her head, and finally towered ten feet above her.

The trees thinned out with every step, so she angled her body to stay hidden. As she neared the site, a voice she recognized raised the hairs on the back of her neck. She peeked from behind a scraggly tree to see Jared strolling across the log bridge as if it were the red carpet at a premiere event. "Good job, my friend."

Jared descended from the log, keeping his back to her. She could only see the faces of Adam and Ruger, and a small part of Quin's dark hair behind Ruger's wide frame. The furious expression on Ruger's face made her chills intensify. Hopefully he wouldn't do anything stupid to get himself killed. A pulse of fear surged through her veins as Adam moved over to make room for Jared. Would he kill them both? With a rush of a different kind, she realized she couldn't lose either Quin or Ruger. Despite his flaws, Ruger had cracked open her heart. With him, she had no need to pretend, no need to justify what she did or how she felt. With Quin, she was safe. But with Ruger, she was free.

Adam pushed his shoulders back, proud. "You were right. These guys tried to steal my aqua." He glared at Ruger. "But I'm sure they've learned their lesson. Right, boys?"

Clearly, Jared hadn't told Adam the real reason they were here.

Beyond Ruger, Quin's dark head bobbed up and down. Ruger, however, kept his gaze fixed on Jared. She could only imagine what ugly things he'd like to do to his brother right now.

Jared held his body stiff. "Kill them so they won't ever bother you again."

Adam shifted on his feet, the gun lowering just a bit. "I don't think that's necessary."

"Shoot them!"

The outburst was so sudden, Adam jumped back. He gripped the rifle with white knuckles. His voice shook a bit as he answered. "I rounded them up. If you want the dirty work done, then do it yourself."

Jared gave a disinterested shrug as he whipped his hand around to pull out a handgun.

Before Adam could blink, Jared leveled it at Adam's chest and squeezed the trigger. The loud shot made her ears ring.

She stared in shock at the small hole in Adam's chest. Adam opened his mouth for a second, but then it went slack. The rifle slipped from his grasp, clattering to the stones by the river as his body dropped to the ground.

Jared kept the gun pointed at Adam while he fell as if making sure he was dead. When Adam lay still, Jared turned his head toward Ruger. In profile, she could see half of his evil smile. "I don't know why people waste time arguing with me. I always win."

Jared raised the gun and pointed it between Ruger's eyes.

"No!" Alyna screamed and dashed forward, but she was too far away to stop it.

At the sound of her yell, Jared looked over his shoulder, but he looked to the other side. He couldn't see her as she ran.

Ruger charged, pushing Jared's gun hand down and shoving him back.

Alyna covered the twenty feet separating them in record

time. Just as she reached Jared, another shot exploded from the gun.

She dropped her shoulder and slammed into Jared with all the force of her momentum. It wouldn't be enough to knock him over, but it would buy Ruger time.

Jared stumbled a step, then to her surprise, smacked his head on the rocky cliff face. He fell back unconscious, landing on the sandy soil with a thud.

After kicking the gun away, she turned to Ruger. He had dropped to his knees, the muscles in his neck rigid. Kneeling beside him, she searched for a wound. His left thigh dripped a few drops of blood on the ground.

"I'm okay." He grimaced as he tried to stand.

Jared moaned, rolling his head to the side. She hadn't hit him hard enough. The sudden urge to finish the job blindsided her. She could claim self-defense, or close to it since Jared would have killed them. The pistol lay only a few feet from her knees. She imagined picking it up, turning the black barrel toward his forehead, forcing the trigger, knowing he would never wake up.

Her fingers itched with a hatred that frightened her more than Jared regaining consciousness. Turning away from the gun, she put an arm under Ruger's shoulder. "We have to go. Quin, help me."

Quin quickly freed himself from the tree and took a second to rub his ankle underneath the cuff. When she glared at him, he came to help. Once Ruger got to his feet, he could put a little pressure on his left leg, but not much. Alyna tore out her hair tie and slipped it over his foot, then up onto his thigh. It would help stem the blood flow a little.

She started to urge Ruger away, but he pulled back. "Wait. Give me the gun."

Alyna hesitated, still not wanting to pick it up herself. Would he kill Jared if she gave it to him? She didn't get the chance to ask. Quin scooped it up.

He took two steps toward Jared, who was struggling to a sitting position. Quin pointed the weapon at Jared's head. Alyna turned away, covering her ears in anticipation of the shot. Her gaze fell on Adam's lifeless body. If only she could have done something for him.

When no immediate gunshot came, her eyes found Quin again. Turning the gun around, he leaned down and smashed the butt of it into Jared's forehead. The thick thump threw Jared back to the ground. "That will keep him for a while. Let's go."

With a relieved breath, she waited as Quin took his place at Ruger's left arm. Given the state of Ruger's leg, they probably wouldn't make it over the log bridge, so they headed up the steeper slope along the river. As they passed the bridge, Ruger looked over at the blue blanket on the other shore. His face twisted in pain that she knew didn't come from his leg. He had just found his mother, and now he would lose her again.

Alyna struggled under the burden of half of Ruger's considerable weight. Their progress was slow, and she cringed every time the coon cuffs around Quin's ankle clanked, even though he'd shoved most of it in his sock. They didn't have the luxury of time or making noise. There was no telling how soon Jared would regain consciousness.

Glancing down, Alyna cringed again at the droplets of blood dripping from Ruger's leg. He hadn't lost enough to stop him from helping, but the strain had to be wearing on him. She looked over her shoulder. The blood had left a crimson trail along the leaves. They had to get Ruger back to their camp to grab the first aid kit and supplies, but they couldn't stay for long because the blood was like a neon sign pointing the way.

An agonizing hour later, they all needed a break. They helped Ruger to the ground and leaned him against a large tree. He panted and grunted with the pain. Alyna met Quin's gaze and, seeing the same fears reflected there, she spoke up. "This is taking too long. Jared is probably already coming after us."

Ruger nodded, his face pinched. "Go on without me." He took another shuddering breath. "Come back when you can, but not if you hear Jared." He locked eyes with Alyna. "I don't want you putting yourself in danger."

This time, Quin nodded. "He's right. If we both go back to camp, I can protect you."

Alyna smiled. She appreciated the gesture, even though Quin hadn't done much protecting so far. Then her smile fell. "Someone has to stay here. If Jared comes, Ruger would be a sitting duck."

"What if we hide him?"

"Please don't talk about me like I'm not here." His protest was weak at best. He needed to save his strength anyway.

She searched through the trees in a small radius, then returned to the men. Ruger's eyes had closed. Hopefully, he'd merely drifted off to sleep. She refused to think about the other possibility. "There's a dry creek bed just over there. We can cover him up with leaves."

She stripped off her sweatshirt and wrapped it around his leg to soak up the blood. As she pulled the knot tight, Ruger woke with a start. After he had looked down to see what she had done, he smiled at her. "I missed a striptease?"

The laugh exploded from her, a needed release. "Not so much. Glad you're still with us, though. Ready?"

He closed his eyes and nodded. Quin grabbed Ruger underneath the shoulders, and she lifted his legs. They carefully stepped through the underbrush, hoping not to leave a trail. By the time they reached the creek bed, she was breathless from the exertion. They covered Ruger in old leaves, sticks, and dirt. The dirt might not be good for his open wound, but the risk of infection paled in comparison to the risk of Jared finding him.

Before she placed the last clump of leaves over his face, she brushed a hand across his cheek. "How bad is it?"

"Eh, about a three." He gave her a weak smile. "On a scale from one to three."

She sighed at his idea of humor. "Stay safe."

From behind closed eyes, he gave her another smile.

She gulped down her fear and led the way north toward camp, taking one last glance at Ruger's hiding place before the trees swallowed it up. She'd left him yesterday, but this time felt different. This time, she didn't know what condition he'd be in when she came back. Or if he'd even be there.

Shivering in her T-shirt, she trudged ahead. Quin offered her his sweatshirt, but she refused. The hike would warm her up, and she had another one she could grab back at camp. Quin kept pace easily beside her. Their strides were well-matched for hiking. Although he was taller, with a longer torso, her legs were as long as his. The hiking might have felt familiar, but the years of friendship between them now felt foreign. She glanced over at his dark, brooding profile. Did she really know this man? Maybe no more than she knew Ruger.

They reached the campsite a silent hour later and quickly went to work. Alyna grabbed a sweatshirt, the first aid kit, and the tools they needed for the trap. Quin rolled up the sleeping bags and blanket and stuffed backpacks with food, which they were running short on anyway.

In a total of ten minutes, they reentered the woods, leaving from the north and circling around to keep from using the same path they took to get there. A short distance away from the campsite, she stopped to wrench the cuffs off Quin's ankle with a screwdriver. By the time they got back to hiking, Alyna's gut swirled, anxious to return to Ruger and patch up his leg.

Along their circuitous route, they picked out a new campsite in an opening in the forest that could barely be called a clearing. They dropped the sleeping bags and other supplies, then made better time on their way to Ruger.

When the dry creek came into view, Alyna walked beside it, searching for the area where they'd left him. She had a hard time spotting the downed tree, but finally recognized the mass of leaves hiding the lower half of his body. She jogged to him and slid down the embankment. His head was free, shadowed under the tree, and as they approached, his eyes locked on to hers with the look of a drowning man latching onto a lifeguard.

She dropped the first aid kit on the ground and knelt next to him.

He beamed a smile at her. "My angel has come back."

His angel? Maybe he'd lost more blood than she'd thought. She swiped the leaves from his left leg and peered underneath. Both her sweatshirt and the leaves were blood-red, just as she'd feared.

With trembling fingers, she untied the sweatshirt and rolled the leg of his jeans up to mid-thigh. The blood smeared across his leg in swirls as if a child had finger-painted all across his skin. She cleaned it with gauze and alcohol. The bullet had torn through the outside portion of his thigh muscle.

She wrapped gauze around the entire leg. Quin held it in place for her while she taped a bandage around the limb, keeping it tight to stop the blood loss, but not so tight as to cut off circulation.

When she finished, she looked up at him. His tanned face had lightened to a pale shade of yellow, making his dark eyes seem even deeper. He stared at her for a moment, his expression unreadable. Then he grabbed her hand and pressed it to his cheek. The rough stubble against her palm and the smooth contour of his cheek under her thumb created a delicious contrast of sensations.

His gaze held hers as he whispered, "Thank you."

Her heart kicked into overdrive, sending pulses of hot blood to her cheeks. If she didn't reclaim her hand, she'd likely bend over to find out what the contrast felt like between his rough stubble and his soft lips. And wouldn't that be a show for Quin. Leaning back to aid her willpower, she slowly tugged her hand free. He didn't let it go easily.

Taking a deep breath, she focused on their situation. She wanted to ask if he was in pain but knew it was a stupid question. "We've found another campsite. Are you ready to go?"

He nodded, attempting to push himself off the ground. She and Quin steadied him as they limped up the dry creek to a place where the bank was shallower. Ruger sat and scooted up backward, then they resumed walking.

Hours later, they reached the campsite, completely exhausted. Alyna opened one of the sleeping bags while Quin supported Ruger, then they lowered him onto it. Ruger leaned his head back and closed his eyes, but the squinted wrinkles at the corners told her he wasn't sleeping.

Sitting down next to him, she tried to steady her fingers. Despite being more tired than she'd ever been, adrenaline still flooded her system. When she glanced over at Ruger, the dark spot of blood bleeding through the gauze made her even more tense. But Ruger had been lucky. Not so for Mr. Schroeder. His frozen face, wide-eyed and terrified, stayed fixed in her mind.

She needed a distraction. Quin had gone to rest on the blanket, his back to them. Ruger's gauze didn't really need to be changed yet and doing so would only put him in more pain. So she grabbed the coon cuffs and a screwdriver, marveling at how she might recently have been tempted to use the cuffs on Ruger to escape. Would she ever have to explain to her mom how she helped save the man who'd kidnapped her? Mom had always wanted her to do something significant. Maybe this was it. Bringing Jared to justice would be the perfect use of her trapping skills. And yet, somehow, she didn't think Mom would approve.

"He just fell down, limp." Ruger's voice shook.

She swallowed hard and looked over at him. He stared at her, his eyes pleading, asking her to make reality different. But she couldn't. They had both seen a man executed right in front of them.

He let out a long sigh. "I had planned on killing him, you know."

He meant Jared, and she knew it, but couldn't bring herself to admit it.

"But then..." A weak cough.

She handed him a water bottle.

He drank half of it before continuing. "But then, Adam. His death is my fault. If I could have already stopped Jared, he'd still be alive." He pressed his eyes closed. "Maybe I should have gone to the sheriff like you said. But it's too late. By the time we get the sheriff, he'll be gone. My mom will be gone."

"Not if we trap him first." She gave him a half smile as she held up the coon cuffs. "These are what I needed from the hardware store."

A spark of hope lit his eyes. "Good, give me the details." His eyelids drooped. "After a quick nap."

She went back to work.

Just when she'd assumed he was asleep, he spoke again, his voice sluggish. "I didn't want to go back to jail anyway for killing him. My mom wouldn't have wanted that." He slowly shook his head. "You, neither."

"What?"

He cleared his throat. "Your dad wouldn't want you to go to jail."

Why would she go to jail? She hadn't done anything. The blood loss was really getting to him.

"I mean, you're not living...like you're in jail."

"Maybe you should just go to sleep, Ruger."

His eyes popped open, and his jaw muscles twitched. "You're living your dad's life." He took a deep breath. "Not your own."

A muscle in her chest pinched. Now she understood what he meant, but she didn't like it.

"You've got to let the veil die with your father."

"I'm not trying to live his life..." Her words trailed off as she realized that was exactly what she was trying to do. The decisions she made for her life centered around the veil—a quest she'd never wanted. But if she let it go, then she'd have to accept her mom was right about her dad's life being insignificant, and probably about her own too. "I'm going to do something important with my life."

"You're important to me."

Her chest muscles relaxed in one big burst, releasing tingles through her whole body. Was it enough to be important *to* someone? Maybe if it were the right someone. "But I can't just wander around my entire life."

He waved a sleepy hand at her. "Come here."

She scooted a few feet closer.

He managed to glare at her. "No, right here."

She moved close until her leg touched the side of his arm. He raised his hand, and using two fingers, he cupped her chin, his thumb brushing her lower lip. He squinted as if he could barely keep his eyes open. His voice came out slowly, but firm on each word. "Alyna, not all those who wander are lost."

The sting of hot tears burned her eyes. She turned away

before he could see them. He dropped his hand, and having made his point, drifted off again.

She tried to ignore his words, but they spoke of a freedom she hadn't thought could be hers. The freedom to wander. Could it suit God's purpose for her life? But wandering hadn't gotten her father anywhere. Her persistent streak kept chasing that train of thought until the irony crashed down on her head—she was trying to prove her mother wrong by proving her right. Even if Alyna discovered the veil and validated Dad's existence in Mom's eyes that would only confirm that his life wasn't worth anything unless he found something. But it wasn't true. If her dad were still here, she'd give him the words Ruger had just given her *You are important to me.*

FIFTEEN

Alyna gave the area on top of the cliff one last examination. Everything was set for the trap. The jump drive hidden, the large tree branch a few feet away from her, and the coon cuffs ready for Plan A. But with a ruthless man like Jared, they needed a Plan B. She walked to the cliff and glanced over the edge. High above the river, the rope net was strung between two trees. Under her feet, a torn piece of blanket marked its location. They were ready. All she had to do was set off the flare. She walked back to pick up the flare gun, but her finger trembled on the trigger. If this didn't work, they would have called their own killer to meet them.

She searched the dense trees to her right. Although she couldn't see him, Quin waited there with the rifle, in case anything went wrong. It was time.

"Wait." Ruger called out from the clump of bushes in front of her.

"What is it?"

"Just come here for a second."

His leg had seemed more stable this morning, but maybe he

needed the bandage readjusted? She crept through to where she'd left him sitting at the base of a tree behind the bushes. Nobody there.

A strong hand grabbed her and pulled her around. She let out a gasp as she was pushed up against a large chest. Her tense muscles quickly relaxed when she looked up at Ruger, then tensed again at the look of desire in his eyes.

"I need to say something." He bit his lower lip.

She opened her mouth to respond, but then became completely distracted by his perfect white teeth torturing his full, soft lip.

One of his hands settled in the small of her back, keeping her close. A pleasant and terrifying hum took over her body. He ran his other hand down her jawline, and this time, she bit her lip.

"I've never met a woman like you."

Was that a compliment? She held her breath as she waited to find out.

"Stunning." His hand brushed her ponytail off her shoulder, then he cupped the back of her neck. "Brave." He leaned a few inches toward her, adjusting to keep the weight off his bad leg. "Kind." He came so close his breath warmed her cheek. "And loves to play in the dirt. The perfect woman."

Perfect? No one had ever called her that.

His tone turned from sensual to serious, yet somehow it was still sexy. "If anything happens today, I need you to know—"

"This is just the blood loss talking."

"Really, you think so?"

She nodded, her gaze trapped by his deep brown eyes, so dark and warm.

"Then how about I stop talking." He leaned in, bringing his lips to hers.

Her nerve endings seared, firing off sparks through her abdomen. The passion in his kiss melted her heart and turned her legs to jelly. His arms held her firmly upright—firmly pressed against his chest. Stubble roughened her chin, but his lips were soft and full. As ripples of desire crashed over her, he pressed in harder, taking the kiss deeper. Nothing was gentle about this man. He was total muscle, all hardness, and completely masculine. Her body responded by molding to his as the last of her reservations crumbled to dust.

When he pulled back, the truth of the moment slammed into her. She didn't care about the fact he'd been in prison or what he'd done in the past. She was falling in love with Ruger for who he was now.

He pressed his forehead against hers and ran his thumb along her chin, almost an apology for roughing her up. "Stay safe."

It was what she'd told him when she left him in the creek bed. She knew how helpless he felt leaving her out there, but confronting his brother head-on while injured wasn't a viable option.

She nodded and turned to go through the trees. When she looked back once, the expression of longing on his face nearly brought her to a stop. She'd love to pretend they didn't have work to do and extend this time together, but they had to trap Jared before he left the area.

Back in her original spot, she double-checked everything again. Satisfied Plan A and B were both in place, she palmed the flare gun and squeezed the trigger. The flare burst through the trees, streaking into the sky with a flash.

For the next twenty minutes, she took slow, measured breaths. The plan depended on her keeping her cool. Even so, she paced in circles for the following twenty minutes.

Then, in the distance, she heard rustling. *Jared.*

She scanned the trees in the direction of the noise. Nothing yet.

Every beat of her heart seemed to slow until she thought she could count several seconds between each one. Muscles tense, she swept her eyes along the trees again. Over there, a wave of branches. She planted her feet and swallowed down a mouthful of air, trying to relax.

But the man who came through the trees was Quin. He stepped out of the leaves with his hands up.

Her heart stopped for a second before kick-starting in a dangerously erratic rhythm. Jared appeared behind Quin, carrying a handgun and the rifle Quin had been holding. An angry red knot swelled on Quin's forehead.

"Alyna." Jared raked his eyes over her from head to toe. "I can understand what Ruger sees in you. So brave." An easy smile spread across his face. He relaxed his hold on Quin. "Except I don't really get what you see in him. Why would you protect someone who killed their mother?"

Her eyes darted away from him as she imagined Ruger in the bushes listening. What would it feel like to hear his brother call him a murderer?

Jared took her hesitation as a sign to keep talking. "Ruger wants to blame me for something I didn't do. That's the only reason I'm out here."

He must not have realized she'd seen him kill Adam and was the one who knocked him unconscious. The image of Ruger breaking down after finding his mother popped into her head. He might be a kidnapper, but he wasn't capable of killing anyone. She turned hardened eyes back to meet Jared's gaze. Let him think she believed him. "Can we get through this without all the drama?"

Jared's grin widened. "Eager. I like that. By the way, where is my baby brother?"

"We're doing this without him." Jared probably knew Ruger was injured, but it was better if he assumed the worst.

"I'll bet he's not far away from your loveliness. I guess we can deal with him after we take care of business. Where is the real jump drive?"

She pointed at a large knot in the tree behind her. "Inside." Stepping away, she gestured for him to reach for it.

He squinted. "At least you didn't put it on a cliff this time."

Obviously he didn't have a very good sense of direction, considering the cliff's edge above the Big Blue Vein was only ten feet away.

He pointed the rifle at her. "You get it."

Her shoulders sagged, feigning defeat. "Fine."

She slipped her hand in, grabbed the jump drive, and handed it to him.

"I'll assume this is the real one since it's not likely you would have a whole pack of black jump drives out here." Suspicion darkened his eyes. "Why did you decide to give it to me?"

She plastered on her most innocent look. "Our lives are more important than justice for the dead." Even though she'd practiced it, the words sounded fresh on her lips. They were truer to her now than Jared would ever understand. "Now you can leave us alone."

He gave an almost believable sad shake of his head. "I can't do that. Maybe if you hadn't taken this so far, but all of you know where the bodies are."

She'd expected this as well. At least he'd given up the charade of being the innocent party.

He tossed his head to the side. "Ruger, I know you're out there. Better come soon, before your girlfriend gets a bullet in her eye." He looked back at her. "Such gorgeous eyes, too. Are they like a peacock-blue?"

She shook her head right back at him. "It was me."

Jared blinked. "It was you, what?"

"I talked them into giving you a chance to do the right thing. Too bad it didn't work." In one quick movement, she dropped to the ground and pulled the rope trigger for the CO_2 cartridges. The pulse of gas pushed out the coon cuff. The one good cuff wrapped around Jared's ankle, closing with a metallic snap.

He yanked on his leg. "What the hell?"

Before he could turn either one of the guns on them, she grabbed the hidden tree branch and smacked it down on his hands. Quin scooped up the rifle as it fell, but Jared had kept an iron grip on the handgun.

Both men turned to point their weapons at the same time.

Quin curled his finger around the trigger. His jaw was set, but she detected the slightest tremor in the muscles. "Alyna, run!" At her hesitation, Quin lowered his voice and screamed, "Now!"

She ducked into the cover of the trees. The plan had always been for her to hide in the trees while Quin kept the gun on Jared, but in that scenario Jared didn't have his own gun—a weapon he was much more likely to use than Quin.

From the bushes, she peered out. Jared scrunched his eyes. Twisting the gun sideways, he shifted his weight from foot to foot, the metal cuff clanking. "What a mess. Should we just sit here until my leg falls off?"

A trickle of sweat slid down Quin's forehead and over his cheekbone.

Jared let out an exaggerated sigh. "This would be so much more entertaining for me if you would just call Ruger out here."

Alyna circled around to where Ruger had been seated at the base of the tree, but he was already gone. She returned to where the other men were in time to see him hobble out from the cover of the forest. He'd taken Jared's bait, and now both of the men she cared about were in jeopardy.

She hovered along the edge of the trees, watching.

"Tell me it was an accident."

Jared put his left finger on his lip as if he was thinking hard. "Define accident."

Fury simmered off Ruger's every muscle, but he didn't move. His lips pressed into a flat line.

"Honestly, I didn't mean to kill her. Who really means to do it their first time? Of course, I'd fantasized about it, exploring the different ways I could do it, whether I would make her beg or curse her out, but I never really thought I'd do it."

Ruger took a limping step toward him, his fists curled tight.

"You want to know the worst part?" Jared leaned his head toward Ruger as if telling a secret. "It was even more satisfying than I thought it would be."

Ruger's face went white. If he hit Jared, it would be a catalyst. Somebody would die. Right now, Ruger didn't appear to care much if he died as long as he took Jared with him.

She slipped out of the woods and touched Ruger's arm. "Don't."

Ruger held his hand to the side, silently asking Quin for the rifle. She met Quin's gaze and shook her head. His eyes drooped in apology as he handed Ruger the weapon. Of course, Quin wouldn't care if Jared died since Jared could still try to implicate him in Phoebe's murder.

The characteristic smug grin returned to Jared's face. This was the confrontation he wanted, the ending he craved. But Ruger couldn't live with killing his brother. She had to stop this.

She stepped toward Ruger, but then was pushed from behind. She stumbled, catching herself on a tree.

In a tangle of leaves and branches, a man with a beard and shaggy hair darted past her. *The claim jumper.*

He held a small ax in his hand. Jared's eyes were drawn to him. In amazement, she watched Jared's face turned pasty-white.

Ruger swung the gun around. At the sight of the man, his jaw dropped, and the rifle went slack in his hands.

The claim jumper moved to Jared's side, holding the ax high

in the air. Before she could think to react, a hushed question from Ruger flipped the world upside down. "Dad?"

How would Dad know where to find them? Ruger floundered for an answer until he remembered the person Alyna had seen. The claim jumper had been Dad? Except there was no way he was trying to jump Alyna's claim. He'd been keeping an eye on them. How much had he seen?

Dad moved to Jared's side, the ax held high, his eyes on Jared's feet. Ruger finally found his voice. "What are you doing here?"

Dad glanced up to meet Ruger's gaze. His eyes were calm as always, focused, efficient. He raised the ax and swung toward Jared's foot.

Ruger jolted forward a step when he realized what Dad wanted to do. "Wait."

The ax clanged against the chain and smacked a rock underneath. Half of the chain split.

Closing the gap between them, Ruger reached for the ax, but he could tell he wouldn't grab it in time. "Don't!"

Another fast blow. One of the chain links split the rest of the way apart along with half the rock beneath. Jared was free.

Ruger scrambled to find the rifle, discovering it was still in his hands. He raised it and pointed it at Jared again. He glanced at Dad out of the corner of his eye. "I know what this might look like, Dad, but you don't understand."

Dad dropped the ax, finally turning his attention to Ruger. "I understand more than you think."

What did that mean?

"You know the one thing that matters more than anything else."

The automatic response from years of father/son talks came easily to Ruger's tongue. "Family."

"Exactly. So put the gun down, Ruger. Let's work this out."

He couldn't be serious. This wasn't exactly a family squabble.

Dad swept a hand toward Ruger. "You are my son." His hand continued on to reach out to Jared. "And this is my son. Brothers shouldn't fight. Family forever, remember?"

Their family motto cracked Ruger's heart a little deeper, reminding him of all he'd lost. *Family forever* wasn't supposed to mean until they killed each other. An unexpected twinge of conviction hit him. That was what he had been about to do—kill Jared. But Jared deserved it.

"This isn't just a random disagreement." Ruger pinned his gaze on Dad. But Dad's expression never changed. If anything his face flattened into a hard piece of marble. Bile twisted and burned in Ruger's stomach. "You knew, didn't you? That's why you wouldn't let anyone mine on the property."

No change in expression. No acknowledgment. It was enough confirmation. His relaxed, efficient, peacemaking father had let Jared get away with murder. "She was your wife."

A ragged breath came from Dad's throat. "She left our family long before the day she died. But this isn't just about her." He slid his feet closer to Ruger. "You won't understand this until you have your own kids, son. The need to protect your children is biological. I had no choice. Better to cut off my own arm than to let someone hurt Jared, or you."

The unconditional love in his father's eyes filled Ruger with pity. Such love without boundaries, without discipline. It had given Jared the freedom he needed to become a monster. "Can't you see how demented he is?"

"I've found my way to forgiveness." His eyebrows rose, dark eyes pleading. "You're a good man, Ruger. I know you can forgive also."

This was totally nuts. They couldn't let Jared kill whomever he wanted and then cover it up. But then again, Dad had only referred to Mom's death. Maybe he thought Jared had done one horrible thing and regretted it.

Before Ruger could ask, Dad advanced on Alyna. "Let me have the jump drive."

The muscles in her jaw tightened. She placed a protective hand over the hip pocket of her jeans. "No."

Pushing back his shoulders to get to his full height of slightly shorter than Ruger, Dad leaned over her. "My dear, if we destroy that jump drive, this would all go away. Jared would feel safe. No one gets hurt. We can all go back to our lives."

Thankfully, Alyna wasn't easily intimidated, and she didn't look convinced either.

Dad turned back to Ruger. "I'll quietly bury your mom in a nearby cemetery."

Dad really didn't know. Ruger stepped between him and Alyna. "What about Phoebe? Or Adam Schroeder? Are you going to bury them next to Mom also?"

For the first time, Dad's calm facade faltered. "What do you mean?"

"Jared killed both of them."

A strangled gasp. "Phoebe, I always wondered..." A wave of panic rolled over his features. "Adam, when?"

"Yesterday at dusk."

Dad's face aged ten years in ten seconds, wrinkles sinking into the crevices of his eyes. "I heard the shots last night, but then I picked up your trail and didn't go any farther."

Ruger suppressed the sudden urge to put his hands over his dad's ears, to protect him from the truth. But there was no protection from something so horrible. And Dad had already done his fair share of hiding his head in the sand. "Adam's body is over near Mom's, by the big aqua vein on our property."

The details of the deed must have convinced him. Dad turned broken eyes onto Jared. "Son, why would you do that?"

Ruger wrenched his gaze from Dad to gauge Jared's reaction. For a brief second, Jared's face went slack, and Ruger thought he might actually consider the question, but then he shrugged and said, "Why not? I'd gotten away with it."

Dad's nostrils flared. "Only because I thought you'd done it out of anger, in the heat of passion. Elaine knew how to push a man. I'd certainly thought about killing her a time or two myself." He lowered his voice. "I didn't want you to ruin your life because you lost control of your temper." A violent shake of his head. "Turns out you were set on ruining it anyway, and taking a few others down with you."

"I couldn't let them leave." Jared lunged at Ruger, striking out with his leg and knocking the rifle to the ground. "Sorry to disappoint, Dad."

Ruger scrambled after the rifle, but Jared stomped on it, pinning Ruger's hand to the weapon. Ruger grunted at the pain, trying to pull back, but his fingers were trapped under Jared's weight.

In one fluid movement, Jared spun around, pointed the pistol at Dad, and pulled the trigger.

"No!" Ruger threw his entire body toward his dad as if he could interrupt the path of the bullet, but it had already hit its mark. Dad fell back against a tree. A tendril of dark liquid spilled down from his stomach.

Jared flew backward as Ruger bowled him over, trying to get to Dad, who was fading toward the ground. Ruger caught him and eased him down. "I'm s..." Dad choked on the word, but he didn't have to finish the sentence. The guilt and shame were written on his face. Dad was sorry for helping Jared.

Fire churned in Ruger's blood. He jumped up and launched himself at Jared who now aimed the pistol at Quin.

"I should have done this all those years ago. You were always a loose end."

Ruger kept his eyes fixed on Jared, preparing for the full-body hit, even as he heard the chaos erupting around him. The crack of a gunshot. Alyna screaming Quin's name. Another body falling to the ground.

Jared was his target, his sole focus. The one who had hurt everyone who had ever loved him. The one who had destroyed Ruger's life and his own. He didn't deserve to live. It was time to make things right.

Ruger drove his shoulder into Jared's side, and they fell to the ground. As they rolled, Ruger caught a glimpse of Alyna lying not far away, blood seeping from a wound in her arm. Ruger's rage escalated as he realized Jared had shot her instead of Quin. Or maybe she had stepped in front of the bullet.

Instinctively, Ruger reached one hand toward her. During his brief distraction, Jared scrambled away in search of the pistol.

Where did the rifle go, and why didn't Quin get it? Quin knelt over Alyna's arm, both hands pressing on her wound. Ruger searched around. The rifle had landed back near his dad. He raced toward it, picked it up, and swung it around.

Jared smashed it out of Ruger's hands using the butt of the pistol. The rifle clattered down, and Jared kicked it away, right into a tangle of wild thorn bushes.

But before Jared could take aim with the pistol, Ruger grabbed his wrists, shoving the gun hand down. Jared struggled, fighting to overpower him, but Ruger had better leverage.

Despite protests from his injured leg, Ruger held his ground. Molten fury filled his every cell, stoking the wildfire of revenge burning deep in his gut. He focused on Jared's tense jaw and corded neck. If only Ruger could wrap his hands around that neck.

"Ruger, Plan B." Alyna's voice carried at a higher pitch, probably from the pain.

He glanced over at her, hesitating, knowing Plan B wouldn't kill Jared. After Adam, Ruger had never wanted to see another death. But then, Jared had tried to kill Dad right in front of him. Everything inside Ruger screamed for Jared's life. Even that wouldn't be enough. Jared would have to die several times over to make up for what he'd done, but his one life was all the revenge Ruger could extract.

Ruger embraced the anger, letting it fuel him, drive him, push him. Right now, it matched Jared's desperate fight to live, but soon Ruger would win out. He refused to give up until he did.

Son.

The gentle word startled him. He knew it wasn't Dad's voice, but still he looked back at his father anyway. Dad lay motionless, the blood crusting over on his shirt, his face etched in pain. His struggle stoked Ruger's frenzy. He turned back to Jared, renewed adrenaline making his arms blaze with heat.

You are not the judge.

The soft voice in his head shimmered in contrast to the ranting screams of anger coming from the back of his mind. He eased up just a little, and Jared swung the pistol around, aiming for his head. He elbowed it away as it went off, the shot vibrating through both their arms.

You are not the judge.

Though gentle, the voice wouldn't relent. Ruger's feet slipped on a pile of leaves. He faltered, struggling to push Jared's hand away when he tried to raise the gun again.

From the corner of his eye, Ruger saw Alyna stretch her fingers toward him. He could no longer hear her voice over the pulsing blood in his ears, but he understood from her lips what she'd mouthed. "Plan B."

She was begging him not to kill Jared, her pleas reinforcing the persistent voice in his head. Alyna didn't want him to do this. God didn't want him to do this. But *he* wanted to do this. With every molecule in his body, Ruger wanted to see that evil grin turn into a grimace of pain, then finally go slack and empty. He knew he could beat Jared, could turn the gun on him...or not.

He had to choose. In prison, he'd chosen God when he discovered salvation was a free gift. God had given him peace, security, and love, and never asked for a thing in return. After prison, God led him to the truth of what happened to his mother. And he didn't blame God for what happened. His mother's death, Phoebe, Adam, those were all Jared, and yet somehow God wanted Ruger to spare him. *Can I refuse the one thing God asks of me?*

Inches away from Jared, locked in a death struggle, Ruger took in everything about his brother. The twitch in his eye. The thump of his pulse in his wrist. The raw hatred in his eyes. If Ruger ended his life, it would consume him. He'd end up no better than Jared.

Pressing his lips into a hard line, Ruger switched from shoving to letting himself be shoved. As Jared felt the resistance waning, he pushed harder. A quick glance back told Ruger the blanket flag was just over his shoulder. A few more feet to go, and they would be at the edge of the cliff.

Hands clenched around each other's wrists, they battled until Ruger's feet were almost sliding off the cliff. Jared finally looked up, and realization swept over his face, followed by a triumphant grin.

Ruger suddenly pushed back, his arms straining. Using his shoulder, he bumped Jared's chest, goading him.

Jared took the bait. He returned the push in a massive shove.

With a quick twist and fast sidestep, Ruger dodged to the right, causing Jared to lose balance.

Ruger spun around and slammed his shoulder into Jared's

back, propelling him over the edge.

Jared's body seemed to hover in midair, along with Ruger's heart, before he plunged down.

Following the fall with his eyes, Ruger held his breath. Splayed out, the taut fibers of the net looked like a gaping mouth waiting for a victim. But would the trap work?

Snap!

Jared hit in the center of the net, breaking the spindly supporting tree branches. His weight dragged it down.

Twang!

As the bottom of the net descended, the branches securing the rope at the top held firm. The net closed in around Jared. The rope mouth pulled shut, locking him in a swinging prison above the rushing water.

Ruger considered throwing Jared a triumphant grin, but his heart was too heavy. Instead, he glanced back at his dad, at Alyna. They had both suffered because of Jared. Alyna simply because she was in the wrong place at the wrong time. She gave him a weak thumbs-up sign. Even that didn't make him smile. It made him want to cry.

For a second, he stood, torn between rushing to Dad or Alyna. He stripped off his sweatshirt, went to Dad, and pressed the cloth to the wound. "Hold this. I'll be right back."

He ran to Alyna, dropped next to her, and buried his head in her soft hair. His rough cheek brushed against her smooth one. "How bad is it?" he whispered, pulling back to look at her.

A lopsided smile. "Eh, about a three."

"On a scale from one to three," he finished for her, covering her faint smile with his lips. The kiss wasn't as much passionate as it was needy. Despite having Quin as an audience, Ruger needed her to know how much he cared. He'd fallen in love with her. In that respect at least, she was the perfect woman in the perfect place at the perfect time.

SIXTEEN

"She needs to go now." Quin's frustrated tone didn't surprise Alyna. He was probably more than a little irritated at Ruger's display of affection. Plus he was afraid for her.

She was afraid for herself and for Ruger's dad. Although she'd love to forget about the pain by staying lost in Ruger's kiss, it would take them a while to get both of them out of the woods and to a hospital. Unlike Ruger's gunshot wound, hers hadn't gone all the way through, and she'd guess his dad's hadn't either. Pulsating pain radiated out like stabbing knives just above her right armpit. This bullet needed to come out, and the sooner the better.

As Ruger pulled his warmth away, she shivered, the tingling in her lips the only spot of heat left in her. He brushed her hair back, the look in his eyes more tender than she'd ever seen. "Do you think you can walk?"

Of course she could walk. The bullet didn't hit her legs. She shifted and rolled to sit up, both men putting hands on her back for support. A swirl of dizziness muddled her head. She waved a hand for them to give her a minute.

Quin rose to one knee and looked at Ruger over her head. "She shouldn't have done that. I didn't want her to."

Anger crashed over Ruger's features in a tidal wave. He glared at Quin, then at her. "Why did you do that?"

She pressed a hand to her aching head. "It seemed like the right thing to do for a friend."

"A *friend* wouldn't want you to."

A grunt was her only answer. It didn't matter what he thought. She didn't need his permission.

Funny how she flip-flopped so quickly between giving in to Ruger completely and trying to get him to back off. She put a hand on his shoulder. "I'll be fine. Go be with your dad."

Ruger ignored her, helping to lift her as Quin kept her steady. The two men circled her back to support her—Quin's arm high across her shoulder blades and Ruger's low and tight around her waist, as if he were staking a claim. Now *that* she wouldn't mind. He could stake a claim on her all day long.

Before she took a step, Ruger looked back at his dad. She pushed his arm away. "Go. He needs you."

She hadn't meant to imply that she didn't need him, but the hurt in his eyes was matched by his confusion. His dad had no right to keep his mom's death a secret. But if Ruger chose to help her, and leave his dad here, it would tear him apart.

While Ruger turned back to his dad, she and Quin took a few shaky steps into the trees, making slow progress. Just as she was about to tell him to pick up the pace, she heard a heavy footfall.

She froze and pointed ahead at the leaves that had started to shake. Ruger must have heard it too. He ran from leaning over his dad to jump in front of them, taking a wide-legged stance. She peered around his shoulder.

Through the trees, the deadly black hole of a gun barrel poked out. Alyna's stomach went rock-hard and the dizziness returned. *What now?* They had left all their weapons by the cliff.

Ruger tensed his shoulders and fisted his hands. She had no doubt he intended to die trying to protect them, but what could he do with just his fists?

As the leaves parted, a familiar face came through. Sheriff Hank.

Had he come looking for her? Or was he Jared's backup? "Why are you here?" she asked.

The sheriff tried to see around Ruger. "Alyna? I'm looking for you. Are you okay?"

Ruger lowered his arms and stepped to the side. Sheriff Hank's eyes narrowed into suspicious slits.

She blew out a relieved breath, ashamed for thinking he could have been involved. "Sort of. Two of us have been shot."

Sheriff Hank glanced at Quin's sweatshirt wrapped as a bandage around her arm and shoulder, then tightened his grip on the gun. His gaze slid over to Ruger. "Who shot you?"

She tilted her head backward. "Jared Westmoreland. He's strung up in a net."

A tiny frown crossed the sheriff's face. "I was hoping Jared would stay out of trouble while out on bail." He pointed the barrel of the gun toward Ruger. "You're his brother, aren't you?"

Alyna reached with her good arm to grab Ruger's arm. "Yes, but he's nothing like Jared."

Sheriff Hank nodded. "You said Jared's in a net?" A faint smile before it quickly disappeared. "A trap designed by you, I imagine."

Not bothering to hide her grin, she said, "Can you please take care of him and also help Ruger get Mr. Westmoreland to the hospital?" She'd hate for Jared to somehow escape after all the work it took to catch him. "Why are you looking for me, by the way?"

"Your mom tried to deliver a satellite phone to your camp and found it ransacked. She came to me frantic."

Guilt clenched tight in her stomach. "I didn't mean to worry her."

"Sounds like she had good reason for it." The sheriff holstered his weapon. "I'll radio in and tell her to meet you at the hospital."

Ruger returned to his dad. The sheriff hurried to help Mr. Westmoreland to his feet while Alyna and Quin started walking again. After a few steps, she called over her shoulder. "Oh, Sheriff Hank, you might want to ask for some backup. It might take a few men to haul in our catch."

Before she disappeared into the trees, she looked back one last time. Ruger caught her eye and gave her a gentle smile. He was proud of her, somehow she knew it, but mostly she was proud of herself. She'd used her skills to stop a murderer and bring him to justice. If only she had any idea how her mom would react to the news.

Alyna's head pounded like a snare drummer gone wild. Her eyes opened to the sanitized white of a hospital room. How did she get here? The events leading her to the hospital came back like a foggy dream. The gunshot wound. A bumpy car ride. Nurses who had refused to allow Ruger or Quin to come with her for treatment. The gurney wheeling her back for surgery.

She looked over at her arm, surprised by the amount of gauze wrapped around it. The shoddy sweatshirt bandage had looked less intimidating.

"You're awake." Her mom came back into the room from the bathroom and sat in a chair next to the hospital bed.

Despite her aching head, Alyna smiled. It was good to see Mom. Then, more memories of yesterday flooded back. She wasn't the only one hurt. "How is Ruger's dad?"

"He's still in intensive care, but they're optimistic."

A wave of relief washed over Alyna. At least Ruger wouldn't lose both of his parents.

Pointing to the bandage, Mom said, "The x-ray showed the bullet shattered upon hitting your bone, and broke off some of the bone as well." Her mom patted her other arm. "It was a long surgery to get all the fragments out and put two pins in, but you'll be okay now."

Alyna started to nod, then stopped as knife-edge pain sliced through her skull. Her throat felt as dry as the desert. Maybe she was dehydrated. "Can I get some water?"

Mom placed a cup of water in her good hand, and she drank eagerly. When she finished, Mom took the cup from her. "Quin told me what happened."

Ugh. Here comes the lecture about the dangers of gem hunting. This time she wouldn't even argue. It was no use.

Mom stared down at her hands, her bobbed locks falling forward to hit her chin. "I'm impressed with how you handled yourself."

Alyna blinked, stunned. From her mother, that was the highest compliment.

"But I don't want to lose you. Promise me no more stepping in front of bullets or chasing murderers."

Titling her head, Alyna considered her mom's request. There wasn't much Alyna would do differently in the same situation, but at least Mom didn't ask her to stop going out into the forest. "I can do that."

Mom raised her head a bit, peering at Alyna through wavy strands of hair. "So how about a nice safe job as a missionary?"

"That I *can't* do. I'm not like you, Mom. I'm not a social creature. I love the mountains. And I don't want to force myself to fit into this mold you have for me."

Mom lowered her eyes again, looking surprisingly defeated. Maybe she finally understood. Or maybe she just didn't want to argue while Alyna was still recovering. Either way, Alyna would stand her ground. God had made her different for sure, but He had His reasons, and she refused to believe He could only use missionaries to fulfill His purposes.

Mom brushed her hair back and stood. "You've got several visitors. I'll send them in."

Visitors. Was one of them Ruger? Or was he in the process of moving on right now? She would forever be a part of the memory of him finding his dead mother. She couldn't blame him if he wanted to bury their time in the woods along with his mother. She wouldn't blame him, but it would still break her heart.

The door opened and Quin walked through with heavy steps, his head down. His dark hair was scraggly, his charcoal eyes troubled.

"What's the matter with you?" She flicked a hand at her shoulder. "I'm fine."

He paced a few steps, tangling his hands in his hair. "Don't ever do that again. You could have died, Alyna."

"Uh...you, too."

"Yeah, but I deserve it."

"No, you don't." Quin tried to speak again, but she held up her good hand to stop him. "You made a mistake. That doesn't mean you should pay with your life." Until the words had left her mouth, she hadn't realized she'd forgiven Quin for what he'd done as a teenager and for keeping Jared's secret. A bright flutter of peace spread through her chest.

Moisture made Quin's eyes glisten like polished black onyx. He gaped at her. Was he astonished at how she valued his life, or was he still wanting to argue that she was wrong?

After a long moment, he murmured, "I'm glad you're okay."

Ruger stepped into the room, and Quin spun around to look at him. She couldn't see the glance they exchanged, but Quin quickly bolted out the door without looking back.

When Ruger met her gaze, he breathed out a heavy sigh. "I just couldn't believe you were okay until I saw you."

He dropped something into the chair, then leaned on the bed, resting his weight on his right hip. His other leg must still be sore. As he placed a hand on either side of her pillow, she met his gaze. The look in his eyes brought her breath up short. A mixture of desperation and desire that melted away any questions she might have about his feelings. His blazing-hot focus on her sent a wave of heat through her veins.

He lifted the corner of his mouth. "You can't understand what hospital gowns do to me."

"Really?"

He laughed. "No, not really. They're awful."

His gaze dropped tentatively to her lips. Slowly, as if afraid he might break her, he leaned down and brought his lips to hers. The surprising heat of his kiss kick-started her heart monitor. She ignored the beeping, instead wrapping her good arm around his neck and doing her best to convince him not to be so gentle.

He tangled his hands in her loose hair before cupping the back of her neck and taking the kiss deeper. Feverish desire raged through her veins, scorching through every other sensation, including the pain. This was better than any medication.

When Ruger pulled away, she fought with the urge to drag him back. But she wasn't in any condition for marathon sessions of kissing. The nagging of the heart monitor settled down as her pulse calmed, and with the calm, there also settled in a deep sense of devotion. She wanted him to look at her like that forever, to kiss her like that forever. Hard to believe she'd fallen in love with the man who had kidnapped her.

He leaned back on the edge of her bed and pulled her hand up, gently placing kisses along her knuckles. "I have something for you." He picked up a box from the chair and presented it to her in his open palm. It was the decaying wooden box.

He shook it and objects rolled around inside like pool balls. "We made a deal."

She smiled and took the box. He'd brought her the gemstones he'd promised her only a few days ago. Now it seemed like a lifetime.

"Thought you might want to use these to fund your research this winter."

After a quick peek inside at the sparkling gemstones, she shook her head and handed the box back to him. "No, they belonged to your mother. You should keep them."

He narrowed his eyes in forced sternness. "They will stay in this room when I leave to let you rest, and I doubt you're capable of chasing me down the hall to return them."

She smiled and gave him a wink. "In that case, I know just how I'm going to use them. To lease a claim on the Big Blue Vein."

A tremor in his jaw, but nothing else to indicate what he might think of leasing the claim to her. Maybe he didn't want to give an opinion without talking to his dad?

He shifted on the bed, never letting go of her hand. "No more searching for the veil?"

She shook her head, hoping her tired voice held the conviction she felt. "Nope. That was Dad's dream. I have to let it go, just like I have to let him go." She blew out a huge breath. It still unnerved her to claim it aloud, but she pushed the words out anyway. "I'm a gem hunter."

"This experience didn't scare you away from the woods forever?"

"Surprisingly, no. And during the winter months when I can't hunt for gems, I've got a plan. I'm going to run my own rock shop."

He teased open her fingers to drop a kiss on the inside of her palm. "I'm glad to hear that because I've applied for a job with a tax firm here in town. I was hoping you weren't going to be leaving soon."

"Not soon." She caressed his freshly shaved cheek. Despite what they'd both been through—maybe because of it—she knew this man was as solid as a rock. His words from yesterday came back to her *Not all those who wander are lost*. She didn't feel lost anymore, but her wandering soul craved a firm foundation. Could she find that stability in Ruger? "I should give you fair warning. I've recently realized I'm a wanderer at heart, and that makes me hard to pin down."

He brushed his hand along her forehead and smoothed her hair, tucking several strands behind her ear. "Alyna, you can wander all you like. But when you come back..." His gaze locked on to hers. "Come back to *me*."

Her mouth went dry. Not trusting herself to speak, she nodded as her whole body floated on a warm peaceful cloud. She could see a future with him—a future brighter than any polished gemstone.

Dear Reader,

I hope you enjoyed this novella. I've always been fascinated by prospectors and how they spend days and weeks alone in the wilderness hunting down isolated veins of gemstones. I would go nuts without anyone else to talk to (talking to myself only goes so far). But as a former geologist, I do understand the love of rocks that drives them in their quest. I hope I represented them well here and left you with the certainty that no matter what God has gifted you to do, you can point to Him while doing it.

Because my mind wanders so much in real life, *Not all those who wander are lost* has become my mantra. I love to explore no matter what I'm doing, but by His grace, God will always be my guiding light, bringing me back to the true center of His love.

May you also confidently know that God loves you and has called you to do amazing things.

Blessings,
Janice

Did you enjoy this story? **Would you like another one for free?**

I'll send you a free ebook copy of *Convicted*—a short story about Lucan Milner, one of the characters from my novel, *Crevice*. All you have to do is tell me where you would like the story sent via email. I value your privacy and would never spam you. You will receive updates on free and discounted books, great book recommendations, plus gift card giveaways, and an insider's look into my writing world.

Visit http://janiceboekhoff.com/free-book/ to get your free story!

One stupid mistake could save Lucan's soul...

Sixteen-year-old Lucan Milner is only trying to impress his twin brother, Chad, when he makes the stupidest decision of his life ... and lands them both in juvenile hall. Inside juvie, Chad turns down a dark path, leaving Lucan to fend for himself.

When Lucan is mistaken for Chad, he's beaten within an inch of his life. In the infirmary, he's visited by a pastor who preaches forgiveness, but as far as Lucan is concerned the score between them is now even, and he wants nothing more to do with Chad.

Then, the warden asks Lucan to risk his life to help his twin. Although it would be easier to harden his heart, Lucan reluctantly agrees. But how far will he have to go to save his brother from self-destruction?

Visit http://janiceboekhoff.com/free-book/ for your free copy!

ACKNOWLEDGMENTS

The longer I write, the more I realize that writing is not the solitary endeavor I like to think it is. Every person I meet, every event I hear about, and every story someone tells me about my cousin's-brother's-sister somehow makes its way into my novels. With that in mind, I would like to thank the whole world...acknowledgments done, whew!

But seriously, I can only thank a few of the people who have meant so much to me on this journey (otherwise this would be longer than the book).

To Todd, my wonderful husband, I literally couldn't do this writing life without you. Your support (both financial and emotional in equal measure) means the world to me. Thank you for giving me the opportunity to follow my dreams.

To my three kids, Zach, Jenna, and Riley, I pray that every day I save my most precious words for you. It melts my heart whenever you tell your friends or your teachers, "Hey, my mom's a writer." Your pride in my accomplishments keeps me working hard even when the words aren't flowing.

To Crystal, thank you for editing this novella, for being my critique partner, and most importantly for being my beloved friend. I'm so grateful to God for bringing us together.

To Mel, what would I do without you to edit my back cover copy or to bounce ideas around or to give me marketing ideas? Your drive and aspirations are an inspiration to me. I'm so glad our writing journeys have happened simultaneously.

To JoSelle Vanderhooft, thank you for your edits.

To Kim Mesman, thank you for using your talents to give me the most suspenseful jewel-toned cover in print. It's perfect!

To my amazing readers, I also literally couldn't do this writing life without you. Thank you for investing your time in my words. I pray that you leave each of my stories somehow changed for the better. Whether it's to see a different perspective or connect with a different person or even just as entertainment to rest your weary soul, I pray these words have met your where you are.

Blessings,
Janice

ABOUT THE AUTHOR

Janice Boekhoff is a former Research Geologist who pours her love of science and the outdoors into her suspense novels. Janice is a three-time finalist in the ACFW Genesis Contest. She writes from Southern Louisiana where she enjoys having only three seasons (cool, warm, and blazing hot). When she's not writing, she's hanging out with her amazing husband and three feisty kids or patrolling her backyard to keep her predator Vizsla (that's a dog, in case you weren't sure) from eating all the cute little geckos.

janiceboekhoff.com
janice@janiceboekhoff.com